THE WAYFARER

Jennifer L. Hayes

Dormer House Press

ISBN: 978-0-692-73048-5

Acknowledgments

While I had lots of fun writing this book, I certainly had lots of help along the way. At the very top of my list of people to thank is R.C. Had it not been for his encouragement I would never have started it in the first place. His knowledge and insights were invaluable. Let's face it, writing a novel can be daunting, not to mention plagued with moments of self-doubt. On that note, my very dear friend Elizabeth Ross comes to mind. Every time I felt ready to throw myself off the proverbial cliff, she was always there to pull me back.

A special thanks to all those who read an early draft of the book: Leslie Blake-Cote, Ellie Lawther and Nikki Lewis to name a few. Your feedback was much appreciated. Ellie's tech skills also came in handy more than once. Last but not least, thanks to my husband and beautiful daughters for putting up with me while I stumbled along trying to do it all.

"Two roads diverged in a wood, and I—
I took the one less traveled by,
And that has made all the difference."

Robert Frost

Chapter 1

Picture Perfect

The muscles in my legs seized violently and I knew I wouldn't make it. I wasn't strong enough. The fire burned in my lungs, the contents of my stomach churned in my belly. I was on the verge of collapse. Maybe even death.

"Faster!" bellowed a female commando-type in a rough English accent. Her hair was cropped short like a boy's and her arms heavily tatted. "Go, go, go, go! Move it, they're catchin' up!"

Who was catching up? My body responded to the panic this woman instilled but I knew I couldn't keep going. I reached for the tension knob on my bike.

"Don't even think of touchin' that!" she yelled at the class. My hand hovered as I contemplated whether I was bound by some sacred spinning rule. "We're almost there, keep up the pace, don't get left behind."

Left behind? We're on stationary bikes, for Christ's sake. I dared a glimpse of the clock on the wall. How much time was left of this torture? We were only five minutes in. Holy shit! I'd never make it.

"Eyes off the clocks, ladies, it doesn't make time go faster!"

How did she keep doing that? She had me on her radar. She must have sensed my resolve weakening. I just wasn't cut out for this.

The woman next to me pedaled like her life depended on it. Sweat poured off her face. How could she keep at it like that? That wasn't me. I was better at coasting than pushing myself. With shaky hands, I rearranged my thick blonde hair in a large bun on the top of my head. Even the slightest touch of it on my shoulders made me too hot.

Mentally I cursed Ben for making me join the gym. He'd said he was worried I'd become depressed by the English weather, coming from Southern California where the only fluctuation in temperature was from sun to more sun.

The real reason, I thought, was that he wanted me to meet people so that I wouldn't be sitting around waiting for him to come home from work every day, calling on the hour to see if he was on his way.

Maybe I was a bit dependent these days. At twenty-four, I was now officially an orphan and that had put my life off balance. He didn't understand that. His parents were alive and well and doting, giving him that sense of belonging you had when you were part of a family, the one you only realized you even had after it was gone. Now I was a drifter. Somehow I needed to find where I could belong again.

I felt a lot of anger towards my parents for dying on me, my mom when I was eight and then my father six months ago. If I had to be honest with myself, he'd died when my mom had and from that day on it had been one tiny death every day. He drank to forget, he drank to be happy, he drank to pass out. I'd tucked him into bed more times than he had me.

It should not have come as a big surprise when he was diagnosed with stage-four liver cirrhosis. He'd died rather swiftly. Apparently, he was lucky to go quickly because those who lingered suffered a great deal, or so I was told. Selfishly, I'd wished for more time. Time to make repairs to our fragile relationship. Time to say goodbye. Time to wrap my head around the idea of being alone. I've come to realize that no amount of time could have helped any of those things.

At least I had Ben. He'd been very supportive in the aftermath as I found myself overwhelmed by funeral arrangements and the daunting task of settling my dad's estate.

Ben's big promotion had come as a surprise. Perhaps even a welcome change of focus from the dreariness of grief. He'd always been eager to return to his family and birthplace. I supposed I needed a fresh start too.

"Increase the tension, people, we're going to climb. It's going to be long and hard."

Sweat dripped off the instructor's toned shoulders as she barked at the class. What a contrast to my own wiry frame. I was relatively tall at five eight and slim, but lacked definition.

Maybe this move to England would be a good time to make some improvements in my life. A makeover of sorts.

Coming back to the cottage, I took in the fairytale cuteness of its thatched roof and small wooden front door. I wondered if seven dwarfs were somewhere inside sleeping. The real estate woman, Miss Evans, hadn't found that funny when I'd asked.

Clearly it wasn't built for someone six two. Ben had to crouch to avoid banging his head. *This will do nicely,* I had thought to myself at the time. The plumbing, we were told, would leave a little to be desired but what could one expect from a two-hundred-and-fifty-year-old cottage?

Ben had grown up in a much larger old home like this, only twenty miles away in the beautiful town of Oxwich. His parents still lived there.

It had been an important market town in the seventeenth century and a main route for anyone heading southwest from London towards Portsmouth. During the railway boom of the 1840's, a train station had been built and tourism had quickly turned the small country town into a popular destination for Londoners.

Our small cottage was part of the Dormer House estate, which sat on a hundred-acre parcel in East Sussex. The stately home, which was only steps from the cottage, sat perched above the chalk hills of the South Downs in the district of Pembrooke. It was idyllic.

The cottage was littered with boxes in various stages of emptiness. I had struggled with what to bring. Coming from southern California, I had very little experience with rain or "weather", so I'd needed a whole new wardrobe.

On a good day I hated packing but boxing up ones entire life proved to be an emotional nightmare. What did you do with all those pointless things that you'd collected over the years, each one saddled with its own memory? I remembered taking out my box of old ribbons and trophies from my days as a competitive horse jumper. I'd nearly forgotten that I still had the stuff. Recounting every exhilarating ride when I'd won the blue ribbons, I'd had to take everything out and organize it in colors. They felt silky in my fingers, but some were faded from the late afternoon sun that used to bathe my bedroom walls. My ribbons had continued to hang in my childhood room long after I moved out. It was only when my father had remarried that my old room had been converted into a guest room and the ribbons had been carefully entombed in a cardboard box.

Most of my books had made the long journey overseas. Ben and I had argued about that. He felt that they were unnecessary to bring as they were so cumbersome and I'd already read most of them. He thought I should sell them or give them away on Craigslist.

"Really, Emma, we don't even know if we'll have room for them," he'd pleaded.

"I don't care if I have to stack them against a wall, they're coming." Tears had stung my eyes. Many of the books had been my mother's. She had been an avid reader who always had a book in her hand. When I'd snuggle up to her on the couch she'd often start reading out loud to me. I really hadn't cared what the story was about—I'd simply loved how her voice sounded when she read. Maybe that was why books had become a passion for me as well. They were all I had left of her.

Now, surveying the mountain of boxes stacked in the cottage's cramped confines, I wondered if Ben had a point. Where on earth would they go?

As if on cue, Ben materialized from the bedroom with his laptop in hand and shot me a knowing smile. Could he really know what I'd been thinking?

The roses he'd given me when I'd first arrived lay parched on the coffee table like limp lettuce. "I knew these were your favorites," he'd said when he'd picked me up from the airport, and all I could think was, *Why on earth would you think that?* I preferred wildflowers. Roses were generic and predictable. I hated their velvety petals. Why after three years didn't he know this?

April, my best friend in L.A., would have told me I was difficult to please. We'd been inseparable since our first day of high school when I'd asked for directions to my math class. After walking in circles she finally admitted she didn't know where to go. For some reason, I found it hilarious and that was the beginning of our friendship.

Maybe she was right. Maybe I did have a problem. As all this went through my mind I'd turned and said, "They're beautiful, thank you."

Now Ben reached me in three long strides and wrapped me in his arms.

"Hey, doll, how was the gym?" he asked as he nuzzled my neck.

"Brutal." The truth was, I really did feel better.

"How are you feeling?" His lips brushed against my neck, the bristle from his stubble sending me squirming out of his arms.

"Still a little foggy, but good," I said, planting a token peck on his lips. He turned from me and walked the short distance to the dining table where he started rifling through a large stack of papers.

Ben was built more like a football player, with his thick, sturdy limbs and wide neck. Not the kind of physique that benefited from his many hours at a desk. Over the last year he'd started to develop a middle-aged paunch around the waist from the lack of exercise. All too premature given the fact he was only twenty-seven.

Ben and I had met in college, dated for two years and then took the next obvious step and moved in together. He was perfect for me. That was what everyone said. By everyone, I specifically meant April, who had introduced us and seemed to be the voice of many.

According to April, he was a ten out of ten compared to anything she'd found on any of her online dating sites. Ben was everything I could have imagined for myself: handsome, relatively sporty, smart and very organized. He even sorted his CD's alphabetically. Some might think it was anal but I thought it was clever. He never had to search for what he wanted because it was right where it should be. That was how he liked everything, in its right place.

I had nursed far too many of my heartbroken friends who got hung up on the wrong man. I felt lucky never to have shared that fate. Ben was the type of guy everyone wanted, that was what April always said. "What more could a girl ask for?" she loved to say whenever I questioned my own happiness. "Really, Em, you are impossible." That was the little voice I heard whenever I felt that something was missing.

So when Ben had decided to move back to England for work, I

couldn't say no. I'd finished my undergrad in English Lit and was now at my own crossroads.

"Will you be okay if I check in at the office for a bit?" he asked now, biting his lower lip, the way he always did when he hoped to get his way or anticipated my disapproval.

"Do you have to? Couldn't you just wait another day?" He'd already taken more days than he'd planned for the move, but I felt sick at the thought of him leaving me here all alone to deal with everything.

"Em, we talked about this. You need to start thinking about what you're going to do. When we decided to move here…"

"I know. I know." I held up my hands in surrender. I didn't want to get into this conversation again. What was I going to do?

"You need to figure out what you want to do with your life. I'm not going to be around a whole lot. My hours will be long." He lost patience with me quickly these days. I was sure the move had been stressful for him. His parents were thrilled to have their golden child close by once again, but now he felt the pressure to live up to their expectations, not least of which was their very large investment in his education.

"Okay, okay. I don't need you sounding like my dad. I've been here less than a week."

"Fine." He turned away to put his laptop back in his briefcase. "How about we check out one of the local pubs tonight for dinner when I get back?" He pulled on his coat and straightened his shirt.

"Sounds good." I softened at the prospect of beer in my near future.

I must have inherited that from my mother, who had been English. She'd grown up near Manchester and what was left of her family still lived in the North, or so I was told. Sadly, I'd never really known her well. She'd died in a car accident when I was eight, but

I'd always attributed my love of beer to her.

"You really should give the roses some water. They are looking a little worse for wear," he said as he headed out the door.

Chapter 2

Dormer House

With all my clothes put away and half of the kitchen boxes unpacked, I decided to take a break. I peeked out the window, watching the rain falling in a gentle mist. With a quick snip of the scissors, the tags fell from my North Face jacket and my shiny new Hunter boots were about to experience their first taste of English weather.

The dilapidated stables up the lane looked ready to topple over. Ivy clung to the walls and windows, and plants had sprouted up between the cobblestones inside. At one time this had served as the main Dormer House stables. I couldn't help but imagine all the majestic horses that had gone through those doors. A much bigger, more modern stables had been built up closer to the stately home. Sadly, there were no longer horses boarding there—I'd asked Miss Evans—only gardening equipment used for mowing and pruning the vast grounds of the estate.

My father had often said I was born in the wrong time. Horses were a luxury now but at one time they had been a necessity. My mother, who was quite an accomplished equestrian herself, had started me in lessons when I was only five. That was the end of Barbies for me. All I'd cared about was horses.

The air smelled of wet leaves and mulch as I made my way up the gravel road towards Dormer House. It was a welcome smell, being conditioned as I was to fear the dry seasons in L.A. because of the risk of forest fires. Beads of water rolled down my hood and dampened my loose strands of unruly blonde hair. As I rounded the thick hedge Dormer House came into view, a sight that instantly took my breath away.

It was the perfect example of a country house, with both symmetry and simplicity. It had a hipped roof with a deep cornice, dormer windows and tall chimneystacks; a central three-bay frontispiece was set slightly forward, with steps up to a pedimented doorway. According to Ben, it had been built in the eighteenth century by the first Earl of Pembrooke. Its use of red brick with stone dressings looked Dutch. The two-story stately home sat above a semi-basement with two rows of four large windows extending on either side of the main entrance. An impressive building even now, it was used mostly as a museum and for special gatherings and elite functions, at least according to Miss Evans, who had filled us in when we'd decided to rent the cottage. It was said to house an extensive library of rare books and first-edition novels. At least a dozen cars were parked in the lot near the front.

Once inside I followed a few tourists to a small table with a donation box. If you wanted the guided tour that set you back ten pounds. I dug out a five-pound note from my jeans, the only money I had on hand, and reluctantly slid it into the box, making a mental note to keep pound coins on hand, as I would be visiting often.

As I made my way around, it quickly became apparent that each room was grander than the last, with their high ceilings and wainscoting on the walls. Elaborate chandeliers hung over a dining table that could seat twenty. On the walls in the dining room were paintings of shipwrecks and hunting scenes.

I followed a trickle of wide-eyed visitors to a large receiving room with a ten-foot fireplace dominating the space. Faces were carved into the marble on either side. Portraits of past earls and deceased family members hung over red flock wallpaper. It was a mixture of both paintings and photographs.

A black and white portrait of a man caught my attention. He had dark hair and piercing light eyes. His sideburns reached down to his cheeks, but he was otherwise clean-shaven. He was strikingly handsome, despite his expression, which was serious and haunting. No one ever smiled in those old pictures. There was a depth in those eyes. A longing, perhaps? "Lord Henry William Drake 1827-1854," read the plaque beneath the frame.

A tingling sensation coursed through my body. The hairs on the back of my neck stood at attention. What was it that drew me into this picture? I wanted to reach out and trace the outline of the man's strong jaw line.

From the opposite side of the room, a small old man with a booming voice and a slightly hunched back approached with several visitors in tow. His nasally English accent brought the word 'posh' to mind. Among the visitors, white Reebok sneakers and gray sweatpants immediately pegged the Americans.

"Here is the portrait of the third Earl of Pembrooke's only son Lord Henry William Drake, who died tragically in a hunting accident at the age of twenty-seven. His body was found on August twenty-second, 1854, by a river bank near the White Hart. There were whispers of foul play, although nothing was ever proven, and the earldom then passed to his brother-in-law," the old man finished in a dramatic voice before moving on to the other side of the room. The visitors all whispered to each other.

How sad, I thought, staring at the portrait once more, as one might look at a body in a coffin during a wake. All done up in their finest, a life cut short; what a waste.

I had been to my fair share of wakes when I had been a child. My parents had thought it healthy to be around dead people. I'd learned the proper social etiquette—looking somber, bowing my head and speaking of the deceased with what I thought were words of solace. Things like, 'They will be sorely missed.' 'He was such a lovely person.' I wasn't sure why I felt compelled to say something, because most of the time I hardly knew them, but it always felt like the right thing to do. However, in this moment I could not summon a single one of my standard clichés. A life cut short was so tragic. He had been the same age as Ben was now.

Afterwards, I had lost interest in searching out the library and decided to leave that for another day. Like an art museum, Dormer House had left me feeling drained and thirsty. In the foyer, or receiving hall as they referred to it, I scanned the large staircase. On the top landing before the stairs spiraled out of sight stood a mahogany grandfather clock. As if on cue, it chimed three times. I stared at it for a moment longer, half expecting someone to appear on the staircase.

The voice of the tour guide echoed through the old house. An older woman wearing a flower print dress bumped into me on her way by, scattering her pamphlets to the floor. Instinctively, I bent down to help her pick them up. When I stood up I swayed a little. Was I having a dizzy spell?

"You all right?" the woman asked with concern.

"Fine, I think. Just stood up too quickly."

Outside, the welcome warmth of the sun banished all evidence of my prior dreariness. Walking away from Dormer House, I felt the light breeze on my cheeks. The crunch of the small pebbles under my feet grew louder. Not only that, the trees and grass were the most vibrant shades of green. A strong sense of déjà vu rushed over me and

I stopped to take it in. Walking again, I thought, *Yes, I did this last time.*

My throat started to tighten and it felt like I had just come off the pitching deck of a ship. Anxiety? It had been a while since my last panic attack, if that was what this was. I let the nausea roll over me and once the floating feeling stopped I walked carefully back to the cottage to wait for Ben.

Chapter 3

The White Hart

The White Hart was a short drive from the cottage. The sun was low in the sky, bathing everything in warm golden light. Inside the old pub, with its low-beamed ceilings and long wooden bar, the locals were settling down with a pint after a long summer's day. The place had a musty smell, infused with fried food and strong beer. Passed out in front of the unlit fireplace, clearly a regular, was a large chocolate Lab.

Sitting in a tiny little booth made only for two, I scrolled through my Facebook messages while Ben ordered at the bar. I took a picture of the Lab and posted it with the caption, 'One of the pub locals.' I knew April would 'like' it right away.

I had decided not to tell Ben about my dizzy spell this afternoon. He'd only jump to conclusions and race me over to the nearest doctor's office, or 'surgery' as they called it here. Maybe worse, he'd feel guilty that my panic attacks were coming back because of the stress of the move. No need to alarm him. I was sure it was just the jet lag, or getting over my period, which had been heavier than normal.

Ben slid gracefully into the bench across from me with a delicious-looking pint in either hand and the number eight tucked under his right armpit. I relieved him of one pint. The coasters on the table read, "The White Hart, established in 1847." I took a picture of that too with my iPhone and posted it to my Instagram. With one hundred and seven followers, there was pressure to keep posting. A Facebook message came through from April.

Aprilhunt: *Holy Cuteness! Miss you already.*

Me: *Can't wait 2 CU in a few days! ;)*

Aprilhunt: *Counting the minutes. xx*

"Are you documenting everything?" Ben always laughed at the ridiculous things I liked to photograph.

"Maybe." I tucked my phone back into my jean pocket.

"What a great place, isn't it?" Ben adjusted the number perfectly on the table and took in the atmosphere of the place. "This was the first pub my mates and I came to." He looked around, reminiscent. "Cheers!" he said and smiled. "To a new life."

"To a new life," I repeated with more enthusiasm than I was feeling at the time.

We clanked our full pint glasses, spilling some beer on the table.

"Do you know why people would say cheers before they drank?" Ben asked with his boyish grin.

He loved little bits of trivia. He always retained the most useless facts. People always felt it added to his charm.

"Because it was polite? Why?" I asked, taking the bait. He'd told me this already on several occasions but I never let on. He liked the story so much I never wanted to spoil his telling of it.

"Because in medieval times, it was common to poison your enemy." He paused to take a long sip of his ale. "And so when you banged your glasses together, a splash from each was supposed to fall into the other's cup. It slowly became a mark of trust."

"Makes sense. I guess I have nothing to worry about, then," I said, smiling and pretending to look anxiously at my beer. "How was your time at the office?"

"All right… I mean everyone was nice and everything…" He paused.

I could sense a 'but' coming.

"… but there is definitely this archaic way of doing things here." He started fidgeting with his coaster while he spoke. "Maybe I've just spent too much time in America. They love to keep telling me, 'It doesn't work like that.'" He put on a posh London accent. His own was more like a Hampshire farmer's, with his f sounding more like a v. He dropped his shoulders. "And how about you? How was your day?" He looked at me anxiously. Was he bracing himself for a complaint?

The last thing I felt like doing was giving him any more reason to worry, so I perked up.

"Great! I walked over to the Dormer House and checked that out. It was pretty amazing. I didn't quite get to the library there but maybe I'll see that tomorrow," I said, excited once again by the thought of it.

Our food arrived. I'd opted for the goat cheese salad, but ended up eating half of Ben's fish and chips. He watched with patience. He never understood why I didn't just order the food I wanted.

I told him about the paintings and artwork at the Dormer House, but his mind was elsewhere. Art had never really been his thing. He understood and appreciated books, but paintings were never very inspiring to him. He was a practical kind of guy and I guessed so was I in many ways. The decisions I made in life were never inspired by passion, but always practicality. Maybe that was why I sometimes wondered if I'd only just scratched the surface of life. What if I made different choices? Deep down I knew that was silly and girlish and naive. Why try to fix something that wasn't broken? I could coast quite comfortably just like this.

Ben was dousing the remainder of his fries in malt vinegar. I hated malt vinegar. I wondered if he knew that.

"So, Em, I was thinking we should get married," he said in the same way one might make a plan to see a movie.

"Oh!" Was this some kind of proposal? I hadn't ever considered the idea. I wasn't sure why. It should have crossed my mind, I supposed, but it hadn't. I certainly didn't have any immigration issues, since I had a British passport. "What is this about? Are you proposing?"

"What? Did you expect me to get down on one knee?" He laughed. "I know you hate that romantic bollocks." Why on earth would he think that? I'd never said that. A little romance might be nice. "I just thought it's about time. We've been together for a while."

I knew I had to overlook Ben's delivery, but did he really know me so little? Could I imagine myself with him forever? April always said I had problems when I griped about Ben. 'Seriously, Em, you are nuts. He's gorgeous, smart and totally into you,' she loved to remind me all the time. So why did I feel hesitant? Shouldn't I jump at the chance to marry the perfect man? Maybe I did have a problem. I was pretty much alone in the world, with no parents or siblings. Other than Ben—and of course April—I had no one.

"Fine. I mean, sure. If you think we should?"

"I knew you'd say that. I've already told my parents. They're so excited. They're going to pop around for tea tomorrow night to celebrate. Maybe you can whip something special up?"

Already I could feel the domestic duties piling up.

"Oh, I almost forgot," Ben continued as he searched his jacket pockets, pulling out a small worn velvety box. "My mom's giving us her great-great-grandmother's ring. I'll just have to have it sized to your finger."

He handed the box to me without ceremony.

"Are you sure? That's such a big deal." Jewelry was a big thing in Ben's family. Pieces were passed down from generation to generation. I opened the box carefully, as if whatever was inside might spring out.

The first thing that struck me was the size of the emerald. It sat flanked by two good-sized diamonds and three tiny ones circling each of those. This ring was probably worth a fortune. Certainly not something we could afford if we had to buy it.

"You should give it a try, Em."

"I'm afraid to even touch it, let alone wear it."

"Don't be silly." He reached for the box, yanked the ring out of its black velvet perch and slid it on to my finger.

The stones were so heavy and the ring so big that it nearly slid right off my finger.

"We'll have it sized to your finger. My great-great-grandmother was a rather large woman. It's a tad garish, but my mum says it's one of a kind."

"I've never seen anything like it," I said absently. *Not like I'm a connoisseur of jewelry.*

I studied the ring, still trying to process the enormity of what this piece of jewelry represented.

A bus boy started to clear our plates, oblivious to the recent proposal.

"What do you have for pudding?" Ben asked him. Our business seemed to have come to an end. My head was still whirling, but not the way I thought it should be.

After dinner we decided to go for a walk. The pub sat right at one of the many trail heads. It was a beautiful evening. The sun was quite low, but still about an hour from setting completely. In this light,

England seemed much less dreary and much more mysterious. I thought of all of the people who had passed through these same towns and woods—royalty, peasants, noblemen and knights. How many of them had also walked through this same spot and felt as I did now? It was an odd sense of connection.

We walked under a thick canopy of trees. The ground was still soft and squishy from the earlier rain, certainly not the hard dusty trails I was used to in L.A., so parched that you could practically spell your name in the dust cloud behind you. On our right, a steep embankment led to a narrow stream that snaked through the forest. They called this area the South Downs. Its forests led onto beautiful rolling hills; farms and towns butted onto each other as far as the eye could see.

"Look, over there. What is that?" Ben pointed to what looked like a plaque mounted on a rough concrete block, something you might find as a grave marking. It was at the bottom of the embankment on our side of the stream.

"Well, only one way to find out." I stepped out, lost my footing and skidded right down to the bottom.

"Em, you okay?" Ben called down, half laughing and half concerned.

With nothing more than a bruised ego I stood up and started brushing the mud and leaves off my back and legs. Not quite the graceful descent I had planned. I'd forgotten how slippery mud could be.

By now, Ben was jogging above me and taking the path that led to this same spot. Reaching the plaque first, I started to read.

"Here the body of Lord Henry William Drake was found on the twenty-second of August, 1854. He was the only son of the Earl of Pembrooke. It was said that after he separated from his hunting party, a stray bullet pierced his chest and he bled to death on this very spot.

His body was later discovered by Mr. Richard Greasly, the owner of the White Hart pub."

The picture. It was like uncovering another piece of a puzzle. I was standing on the very patch of dirt where that handsome young man had lost his life. My eyes started to well up for no good reason.

A twig snapped beside me and without looking I knew it was Ben.

"So, who's died then?" he asked, looking at my somber expression. He knew I cried easily. Often he even teased me about it.

"It was the man in the picture I saw today, the one I told you about from Dormer House. The earl's son." I brushed at the rogue tear. "This is where he was found." I touched the plaque gently, as if to soothe the soul lost here.

"Ouch!" Ben was reading over my shoulder. "Bleeding to death is not on my list of ways to go." He was trying to be funny.

"How *would* you like to die?" I asked with as much sarcasm I could muster.

"In bed, with the love of my life," he said and snatched a quick kiss before I gave him a playful shove.

Was I really the love of his life? More importantly, was he mine? My heart never leapt out of my chest when I saw him, but did that mean it wasn't love? When we kissed, it was nice but not the passionate embrace you read about. How was what we had different from anything else? How did one measure love? Strong friendships often led to lasting, loving relationships. Didn't they?

"Shall we?" he said, reaching for my hand.

"Yes, I guess it's starting to get dark," I said, brushing some dirt from my jeans with my other hand.

On the way back to the car I couldn't help but imagine how terrifying it must have been for that poor lord to die alone in the middle of the forest.

Chapter 4

The Storm

I decided to bike into town to get groceries for the dinner I was tasked with making. Ben had offered to leave me the car when he went off to work, but there was no way I was ready to drive on the wrong side of the road.

The sun was high and bright. Puffy clouds dotted the sky like sheep grazing in pasture. Even in August the weather here was so unpredictable, so I threw a baggy white t-shirt over my leggings, slipped on some ballet flats and grabbed a shawl just in case. My engagement ring was tucked back in its box on the dresser. There was no way I was going to risk wearing it until it was sized.

Rifling through my things, I found my small brown leather Marc Jacob bag that fit across my body. It had been a splurge at the time, even on sale, but it had since become a well-loved and well-worn accessory. There was just enough room for my iPhone, ID, a small wad of twenty-pound notes and my short little list.

I texted Ben.

Emma: *Heading to the store, LMK if you want anything. xx*

Ben: *No thanks. I'll pick up wine on my way home. ;)*

I found the bikes exactly where our landlady, Mrs. Grimshaw, had said they'd be: in the dilapidated barn at the bottom of the drive near Dormer House. They were covered with a blue, spider-infested tarp. So after careful inspection for extra passengers, I set off riding the bicycle with the cute little basket perched on the handlebars. It was an old rickety thing that rattled whenever I tried to pedal faster.

A short ten-minute ride later and I was in the small village of Foxford, which was comprised of a main high street and an old town square. A statue of a man on a horse overlooked the Tesco Express corner store. Across the street stood the old stone church, St Mary's. I looked around for somewhere to lock my bike but realized that not only did I not have a lock, the likelihood of someone wanting to steal this old thing was slim. So I simply rested it against the red phone booth clearly left as a tourist attraction.

"Good day, luv," said an older gentleman in a green apron, unloading some produce boxes. "Can I help you find anything?"

"No, thanks, I'm good. I just need a few things," I said, digging into my purse for the list I'd scribbled earlier.

After a meandering tour of the store I had everything to get us started. I lingered at the jams and cheeses. Who knew there were so many variations of cheddar cheese? Even the fresh produce could hold its own against any of the L.A. farmers' markets. And of course the bread choices in this small shop could easily rival some of our best bakeries back home. Without realizing, I killed twenty minutes deciding between the buttery taste of Hobnobs and digestive biscuits.

"That'll be fifty-seven pounds and nine pence please." The same clerk also ran the cash register. "Hope you brought your brolly. Looks like rain again."

"Really?" The sun had been shining when I'd biked out here, but looking out, I realized the man was right. In the short time I'd been in the store the clouds had moved in and it was already starting to drizzle. "Bloody hell!" I blurted out, much to my horror. It was the curse my mother always loved to say—that and 'Jesus Christ'. Once she was gone I'd found myself using it here and there. Not the sort of thing you expected to hear out of the mouth of an eight-year-old, and certainly it hadn't gone unpunished, but in a strange way it always reminded me of her and so it had become my go-to phrase.

The clerk looked mildly scandalized. I blushed, and made a mental note to watch my potty mouth. It wasn't even that bad a word. Imagine if I'd said 'fuck'.

I would need to make a break for it before the heavens opened and the bread and cereal I'd just bought turned to soggy mush. Putting what I could in the basket and attaching the other two bags to the handlebars, I set off the same way I'd come.

Just as I got to the end of the high street the rain came down harder. Loud thunder clapped overhead and the sky lit up right on its heels. The storm was directly above. For a moment I was unsure whether to find shelter. If I hurried it wouldn't take more than five minutes to get home but if I waited who knew how long it could last? I pulled my shawl over my head and sped up around the first corner.

Now on a winding country road, I pedaled as fast as I could, my feet slipping on the slick pedals. If only I'd accepted Ben's offer of the car. How hard could it be to drive on the other side of the road? Thinking of that, I should probably switch to the opposite side of this road as I neared a blind corner. The tall hedges on either side made it impossible to see vehicles coming around the bend ahead. While the road was technically two lanes there was really only room for one car to pass.

No sooner had I made this realization than a car materialized right in front of me, leaving no time to react.

I was aware of the impact but I didn't register any pain. My body was thrown through the air. The world spun around me in a blur. Again thunder clapped directly overhead. The whole sky lit up like the sun had burst through the clouds. My nose hairs burned with the smell of sulfur. Every inch of my body tingled from my toes to my fingertips, as if I had been standing on a train track moments before impact. It was a sort of vibration. There was a tugging sensation on my arm. The shrill sound of a panicked horse was the last thing I heard before the back of my head hit something hard.

Everything went black.

Chapter 5

A Ghost

The distant sound of horse hooves on a gravel road was the first thing I heard. A horse? Had I been hit by a horse or a car?

My eyes opened, but it took a while before they could focus. I found myself in a room that I didn't recognize. Beige velvet wallpaper adorned the walls. The mahogany four-poster bed which I was lying in faced a marble fireplace, unlit but brimming with coal. To the right of the bed stood an ornately carved wooden dresser, on top of which sat a porcelain jug next to a white ceramic bowl. Where on earth was I? Paintings of country scenes and still-life fruit bowls or flowers hung all over the room.

What a strange-looking hospital room.

As I peeled back the heavy layers of covers I was wearing a long white nightie. The back of my head was tender and hurt to touch. My hair was a wild mess of dirty blonde locks.

Suddenly pain bloomed. My head throbbed in waves. Under the long sleeves of the nightie my right upper arm was bandaged. Carefully, I peeled back the cloth to reveal a neatly sewn wound about two inches long. Dried blood crusted around it.

My head started to feel woozy. Where in the hell was I? This was definitely not a hospital. I tried sliding out of bed to steal a glance out the window, but my legs gave way and I landed on the ground in a heap.

There was a shuffling of feet outside my door and a light knock. "Miss, you all right? I heard some almighty racket. Are you decent? May I come in?"

"Err... yes... come in," I replied while trying to get to my feet. My legs wobbled and I had to clutch the bed frame to help hoist myself up.

All of a sudden sturdy arms guided me back to bed. "What have ya gone and done?" There was more accusation than concern in her tone. "Lord Henry will be pleased that you're awake," she said while tucking me back into bed like a small child.

She was a short, stout woman with orange curly hair tucked back in a bun. Short stray hairs caught the light from the window, giving the illusion of a halo atop her head. Her cheeks were flushed from the exertion of hoisting me up.

"Where am I?" Bile rose in my throat. I swallowed it. It felt like a bad hangover.

Sympathy washed over the woman's expression. "There's been an accident, miss, and Lord Henry... well, he brought ye here to Dormer House and, well... he'll want to have a word with you 'bout it. Oh, he'll be glad to see y'awake, he will." She poured me a glass of water from the pitcher as she spoke. "I'm Miss Barnsby, should ye need anything, dear."

"Thank you," I said, accepting the glass gratefully.

For the first time I noticed her old-fashioned maid's outfit. It was a dull gray color and grazed the floor. Had she really said what I thought she'd said?

"Am I really at Dormer House? I didn't think people actually lived here."

"Well, of course they do, dear. This is the Earl of Pembrooke's home, why wouldn't he live here?" she said, almost laughing. "Of course, they spend part of the year at their townhouse in London, but they're here every year during late summer and through the hunting season. You rest up now, miss, and I'll go fetch Lord Henry."

With that she turned and shuffled out the door.

None of this made sense. How was this possible? The woman who had rented us the little cottage had clearly said this was now a museum, not a residence. Ben was probably worried sick. Did he even know where I was? My purse was nowhere in sight, which meant it was most likely still out on the road and soaked from the rain. Ben had told me to get one of those Lifeproof cases they claimed were waterproof and now I wished I had listened. The next time Miss Barnsby appeared I would have to ask about my things. If my cell phone wasn't damaged by the rain or the accident, I would need to text Ben.

Sliding out of bed more carefully this time, I used the sturdy posts to keep me steady.

There was an armoire on the other side of the room near the window and I wondered if my things might be in there. The wooden door opened with a creak, so I handled it cautiously, not wanting to make any noise. All I could see were long old-fashioned gowns. Were these costumes? I hadn't noticed any actors walking around in nineteenth-century clothing when I'd visited the other day. From the window I noticed the familiar slope of the hill overlooking the South Downs. My room was clearly facing the front of the great house. However, I couldn't make out the visitors' parking, which should've been there. A small leather-bound book on a side table caught my eye. It looked worn from use, a book of poetry published in 1836. An inscription on the inside of the book jacket read:

To my dearest Henry, may you always enjoy the love of reading. Most affectionately, Mother.

I instinctively flipped through the book and started to read through the first poem when I heard another knock on the door. My heart jumped in my chest and I made a silent dash back to the bed, afraid to be caught snooping.

"Come in," I called out as I settled myself under the covers.

A tall, handsome, dark-haired man in his late twenties appeared, wearing what looked like riding breeches and tall boots with a tan leather top. His white blouse had loose-fitting sleeves tapered at the wrists. He wore it neatly tucked into his breeches with a dark burgundy vest over that. A dark necktie completed the outfit. English country fashion was definitely something to be admired. No one here slogged around in stained sweats and running shoes like they did in the States.

"Madame, I apologize for the intrusion." His speech was proper and his intonation was like music when he spoke. He cleared his throat and looked around uncomfortably. "But I wanted to inquire about your wellbeing. How are you feeling?" He stood rigidly holding a black leather bag. It was the shape of one of those old-school lunch boxes with the rounded top and handle.

"A bit groggy, but fine, I guess," I said, uncertain why this stranger looked so concerned.

"Miss Barnsby informed me that you were up and I wondered if you'd allow me to check your bandages." He hesitated for a moment. "Might you have any objections?"

His sideburns were longer than I'd seen anyone wear them in a while. There was something familiar about him. I knew that face, those eyes. With the sun blasting in from the window their color had suddenly gone from an intense blue to a watery baby blue. I couldn't peel my gaze away from them. They were beautiful and kind. An intense feeling of recognition wound its way through my mind like a pleasant dream. Where did I know him from? I'd only been in town for a few days and hadn't really had time to get to know any of the locals. Aware that I had probably been staring too long, I looked to the bag.

"Oh… are you a doctor?" Feeling slow to catch on, I pushed myself up in bed with some difficulty and started to pull up the sleeve of my nightie.

"Not exactly, madame. Lord Henry Drake of Pembrooke at your service." His smile turned instantly to a look of concern as I imagined I had turned several shades of gray before going completely white as one might when they had just seen a ghost.

"I do have some learning in the matter, and when I was unable to reach a doctor due to the storm I tended to your injuries myself," he stammered.

This had to be a dream. It had to be. When I didn't speak he moved towards me cautiously. "May I?" He pointed at my injured arm. The only thing to escape my lips was a nervous laugh, like the token gesture you gave someone when they'd used a pun that was truly not funny.

I held my eyes closed for about ten seconds and when I opened them again, Lord Henry was staring at me like I had just gone mad as a hatter.

"Please pinch me. I know I'm dreaming. None of this is real."

The bag he had been holding was placed on the side table next to the bed and he looked down at me like a parent trying to explain there were no monsters in the closet. With nothing more to lose, I reached out and pinched Lord Henry's arm and he yelped like a dog.

"Madame?" He look more stunned than angry.

A tingling awareness started at the base of my spine and began to work its way up. This did not feel like a dream. I had heard once that one thing you couldn't do in a dream was read… but I had just read a whole verse from that book on the table. My throat started to tighten.

"Just had to check you were real, that this was..." My voice trailed off. What more could I say? If this wasn't a dream then either I was insane or... I wasn't sure what the *or* could be.

"Are you satisfied? Please warn me if you have the desire to do that again so that I might prepare myself." Lord Henry looked slightly amused. "Now, may I have a look?" Without waiting for a response—perhaps he felt I was completely off my rocker and the sooner he was through with me the better—he set to work undoing my bandage.

My mind continued to race. What had happened to me?

"Lord Henry," I said, reluctantly playing along. "Can you tell me what happened exactly? Was there some sort of accident?"

He stopped with my question.

"I am dreadfully sorry, madame, but my driver said you just appeared out of nowhere. It all happened so quickly. I'm afraid I was sheltered inside from the rain and could scarcely see anything from there. One of the horses whinnied before I felt the carriage come to a sudden halt. I was pitched out of my seat by the crash."

His eyes met mine and I could see how terrible he seemed to feel. He had a small red bump on his right temple.

"Your carriage? You mean with horses?" I had been so sure that a car had hit me, but I had heard horses too.

"Yes, with horses." He looked at me sideways as he resumed his examination of my arm. "I am led to believe by your accent that you are from America?"

"Yes, Los Angeles, born and bred."

"Los Angeles?" He said like it was a foreign word. "Sounds Spanish. Is that perhaps on the west coast of America? I believe there to be Spanish villages on that side?" He examined me a little more closely. "You're certainly a long way from home."

His fingers were large and strong but surprisingly gentle as they traced the line of the stitches. His touch sent a jolt of electricity firing through my body. Every nerve ending awakened.

"Farther than you know," I said, but the full ramifications were lost on him.

The less I got into the details of my being here, the better, until I could figure out where here actually was. He dabbed at the wound with a small piece of cloth.

The fine hairs on my arms and neck stood at attention. I could have stayed under his care all day if need be.

Satisfied with his handiwork, he opened a small metal container and dipped his finger into a clear goo. He applied it to my arm. Noticing how calm I'd become, he spoke gently, kind of like someone might speak to a frightened animal.

"Is there someone we may contact to let them know you are safe?" His eyes searched mine.

Now the panic rose from my stomach to my throat. What was I supposed to say? My words came out in more of a croak.

"Ummm… I don't know," was pretty much all I could manage.

His composure changed slightly. "Have you no recollection, madame? Do you not know where you are lodged?"

"Very little. I really don't know how I ended up here." Which was the truth and until I did know I couldn't commit to anything else.

"You've been out for a whole day. It might take some time for your memory to come back, but the…"

"I've been asleep for a whole day?" I interrupted. Ben. He must be worried to death.

"When I spoke with the doctor this morning he felt it was best to let you rest. As you have been unable to supply us with your name"—he paused and looked anxiously at me—"I have canvassed the nearby estates for someone in search of a missing person. If you are able to supply me with your name, maybe that might help with my search."

His voice trailed off but he waited.

"Emma." It came out a little softer than I had intended. I cleared my throat self-consciously. "My name is Emma Clayton. That's pretty much all I know." What else could I say?

"Lord Henry, at your service. My father is the Earl of Pembrooke. I apologize for this dreadful accident, but I promise to see you right. Consider Dormer House your home until I can reunite you with your family." Lord Henry stood and headed towards the door. "I shall send word for the doctor now, Miss Emma," he said before leaving.

And you are the man from the portrait, in flesh and blood. My brain struggled to make sense of this. I wasn't sure whether to laugh or cry. It was an impossibility, a WTF sort of situation. What the hell would I do now?

Chapter 6

Ruffled Feathers

I woke to the sound of someone moving around my room. My eyes shot open. I expected to see Ben, but it was Miss Barnsby arranging some clothes in the armoire.

"Oh, you're up, miss?" she said without a hint of sarcasm. She had been making enough noise to raise the dead. "I took the liberty of bringing you some clothes from Miss Isobel's closets, as you're about the same size. She won't mind a wee bit, she's still up in London. Your own clothes, I'm afraid, must have been severely damaged in the accident, as you arrived only in stockings and a chemise." One of her eyebrows was raised in question, waiting for me to confirm her suspicions.

If I hadn't felt so drained from worrying all night, I would have felt compelled to agree just to avoid judgment, but as it was, I couldn't be bothered. Let her think what she wanted.

During the night I had convinced myself that if I could fall asleep I'd simply wake up and realize this was in fact a dream, but clearly that tactic had not worked. My purse was nowhere to be found. I needed to go looking for it. If I was in fact in the mid-nineteenth century, what would happen if someone were to find it? The only thing tying me to the purse was my picture ID. What would they make of that?

"Thank you, Miss Barnsby," I managed and I slid out of bed to stretch. My legs had regained some of their strength.

"You must be quite hungry. How about I help you dress and you come down for tea?" she asked through pursed lips.

It did feel good to be up. I was bound to get bed sores if I spent another second horizontally inclined. The doctor who had come last night, Dr. Bainbridge, had been quite useless. He suggested that I remain in bed for the next few days in case I suffered from any dizzy spells.

"I think I can manage myself," I started to say, but looking at the unrecognizable bits of clothing laid out, my conviction floundered. How would I know what to put on first?

She was already at the door.

"On second thought, Miss Barnsby, I could use a hand. I still feel a bit wobbly." I was suddenly grateful for her offer.

She turned towards me and gave me a tight smile. Clearly winning this woman over was going to be a chore.

First, we started with a thin muslin chemise she referred to as a shift and some drawers, which I gathered were supposed to be like underpants. Then, after wrenching me into a corset, she began by layering me up with petticoat after petticoat until I counted six. Finally she helped maneuver me into a simple pale green dress with puffed sleeves and an ornate flower trim. How did women eat or breathe wearing these clothes? Not to mention deal with the summer heat? My shoes had miraculously made it unscathed and I was relieved to be afforded that one little bit of comfort.

Miss Barnsby also offered to put my hair up. I would have stuck it in a pony tail, which would have caused some form of scandal, I was sure. The truth was I had never been very good at being a girl, so hairstyling was not one of my strengths. When it became clear that Miss Barnsby's desire to help me was more out of fear that my grooming could in any way be a reflection on her, she changed her attitude toward me. In turn, I made a mental note of it.

As I came down the wide staircase Lord Henry was just coming in from outside. My stomach lurched into a nervous knot. He was still in breeches, but was now wearing a double-breasted waistcoat, shorter in the front and longer in the back. In his hand he carried a top hat made from felted beaver skin. He caught a glimpse of me and bowed his head.

"Miss Emma, how are you feeling? It's good to see you on your feet." He looked surprised to see me walking around and not completely at ease with it.

"A hell of a lot better, thank you." His eyebrows shot up. Oops. Again with the language. "I thought I'd grab some tea and get some fresh air," I said as I continued following Miss Barnsby towards the dining room.

Lord Henry watched me with amusement.

I was just about to follow Miss Barnsby right through the doors into the kitchen and servants' quarters when she turned towards me. "Oh, you need not follow me, dear, you may have a seat over there and the footman will bring you some tea," she said with a touch of condescension and pointed to a long formal dining table.

The only one in the room to witness my mild humiliation was Lord Henry, who seemed to be waiting for me to sit before he could settle down himself to read some kind of newspaper. He chuckled to himself. My cheeks and ears burned. Within seconds I would be the color of cheap blush. When I was young, everyone had thought my rosy cheeks made me look healthy, but as an adult it had become quite a curse. One sip of alcohol and I was the color of a beet. Every emotion, shame, excitement, embarrassment was reflected by the many shades of red. Who knew there could be so many? There was no hiding with my skin.

Looking around the room with its thick draperies and delicate gold-trimmed furniture, I had always imagined a house like this bustling with people and servants. Where was everyone?

As if on cue, two young house maids bowed at Lord Henry and continued through the room, no doubt on their way to clean something. A footman came through a hidden door with a tray of tea and biscuits. He was dressed in a black tail coat and a crisp white shirt and neck tie. On his hands he wore white gloves and his hair was neatly combed back. He couldn't have been more than seventeen years old but he was surprisingly tall.

He laid a flowered tea cup and saucer in front of me and poured my tea in silence. There was a small creamer and a bowl of coarse-looking sugar cubes laid out beside me.

"Please ring if you would like anything else, miss," he said politely and vanished to the back of the room. I examined the small bell he'd left on the table beside me. He'd meant that literally. I had to fight the urge to ring it.

An uncomfortable silence filled the room as I sipped my tea. Now what? Was I supposed to make conversation with Lord Henry? Times like these having an iPhone would come in handy. Every empty silence could be filled up by scrolling Facebook or Instagram. With the swipe of a finger I was always able to go from Nellie-no-friends to looking busy. It felt excruciating to be without my third limb. Now, without my twenty-first-century distractions, my head whirled as I tried to make sense of my situation. I knew where I was, sort of, but when exactly?

Glancing up, I noticed Lord Henry watching me suspiciously from behind his newspaper at the other end of this long table, his hair catching the light perfectly like a magazine ad. The man was fastidiously well groomed. He had either a very attentive valet or a borderline compulsive disorder. I'd never laid eyes on anyone so well put together. Even his fingernails looked neatly buffed as he held the paper.

His paper.

I snapped back to reality. There would be a date on it somewhere. Reluctantly, I picked up my tea cup, holding it with two hands like I would nurse that first morning coffee, and walked over towards him. I was concentrating so hard on not tripping on the front of my dress that I didn't notice his amused expression as I approached. *My hands.* I quickly readjusted my grip on the tea cup to something a little more dainty, or so I hoped.

"Um... Lord Henry?" I said tentatively. "Would it be all right if you, or someone, maybe your coachman driver guy"—what was the right term? —"could show me where we had the accident so that..." I was trying to catch a glimpse of his paper. Where did papers put the dates back then? Top right or top left?

"Do you think that might help you remember something?"

"Exactly." I still wondered if it would be rude to ask if I could see his paper. His eyes followed mine to the paper.

"Oh, this would be of no interest to you, I'm sure, but I could have Miss Barnsby bring you some books on poetry and womanly things, if you'd like?" he said dismissively. It touched a nerve.

"Wow, that's awfully presumptuous of you to assume that my 'interests'"— I air-quoted—"would be so narrow." I wasn't looking to pick a fight. The truth was I did love poetry but I wasn't sure what 'womanly things' meant. The idea of it brought up my feminist hackles.

"Have I offended you?" He looked confused.

"You've insulted me." As soon as I said it I realized that I should have just let it go. The stress of my current predicament was making me more sensitive.

"Well, I have yet to meet a woman whose interests go beyond such things," he said. "Certainly one with any proper breeding." This last bit was said more quietly under his breath but with a hint of sarcasm. "Pardon me, madame, I don't wish to insult you."

"Apology accepted."

Instead of looking annoyed with me, as I thought he might be, he cracked a smile.

"When you're done with your paper, may I see it?" With my teacup in hand, and not in a dainty way, I walked back to the other side of the table feeling like I might have ruffled a few nineteenth-century feathers.

"Of course, Miss Emma." He drained his own tea, rose and walked the paper over to where I was settling down to inhale those delicious-smelling biscuits the footman had brought me. "You can have it now. I have some business to attend to anyway."

He paused for a moment and looked down at me, sitting there with crumbs on my lips.

"I will have the groom tack up some horses." He paused. "I'll take you to the accident site myself. You can ride, I presume?"

At this I did manage a smile. All the doom and gloom I had felt last night instantly evaporated with the idea of riding. It had been a few years and I'd missed it.

Lord Henry bowed to me and took his leave.

When he was completely out of the room and my daydreams of galloping through the rolling hills had faded, I stole a glimpse of his paper. One of the headlines read, 'Cholera is back in England'. The article listed the many ways to help prevent the spread of the disease; observing the strictest levels of cleanliness at all times was at the top. Further down the page I noticed that Parliament was trying to pass a bill that would allow women to claim spousal abuse as a reason for divorce. Women's lib was still a long way off. Realizing that I was distracting myself, I scanned the paper for what I really needed to know and there it was in black ink—the date.

The Seventeenth of August, 1854.

Chapter 7

Angus

I eyeballed the gown I was expected to ride in and immediately felt nauseous once again.

"I'm supposed to ride in that?" I pointed to the dress, or riding habit as Miss Barnsby called it.

"Would you prefer another color, Miss Emma?" said Miss Barnsby with the patience of a Post Office clerk at Christmas.

"Can I not just ride in some breeches?" We had already been over this.

She chuckled as if I'd completely lost my mind.

In the end, we settled on a pair of pants disguised as a dress with extra folds and a cute tailored leather jacket. While it was summer it wasn't a particularly warm day. It had been ages since I'd last been on a horse and my wardrobe was doing little to help my comfort level.

When I got downstairs, a wiry man of maybe sixty with sharp, skeletal features and a dark suit with long tails approached me. He explained his name was Phoebus, the butler, and Lord Henry was taking care of some urgent business and would join me in the small drawing room in about ten minutes.

"All right, but I'd really love to get some air. Would you let him know that I'll meet him down at the stables instead?" I was anxious to be with the horses and something that was at least familiar. While people's manners, language and customs changed over the centuries I doubted that horses were any different.

The butler's eyes widened, but before he could coerce me into staying I started for the door. He scrambled to get there first, no doubt moving faster than he was used to, his combover hair flapping wildly.

"Ah, madame, may I suggest…" he stammered, perhaps not sure how forcibly he should detain me.

"If you could just point me in the right direction that would be great. I mean lovely." I smiled, hoping that kindness would do the trick. I couldn't tolerate the idea of spending one more second indoors.

"Um… of course." He looked over his shoulder for reinforcements, but none could be found.

I had a pang of sadness when I walked down the drive and saw the little cottage. My cottage. Almost unchanged.

Ben.

Tears welled up in my eyes and I dabbed at them with the gloves that Miss Barnsby had given me. Was he worried about me? Did he even exist at this moment? Technically no, I supposed. Would I ever see him again? How? I had too many questions and no answers.

The only thing I did know was that if I was going to see him again I would need to survive long enough to find my way back home. There had to be one. *My purse.* The only link between me and the future. It could be dangerous if it were found by anyone else. What would they make of its contents? My throat started to tighten and a wave of nausea washed over me.

Breathe, I had to remind myself.

A cacophony of activity from inside the stables refocused my thoughts. Horses kicked and whinnied as their lunch was being served. The run-down building of the future was now a pristine structure. The familiar smell of manure and horse dander was a comfort. On noticing me, a middle-aged man and young boy scrambled to their feet, clearly not used to anyone barging in on their turf.

"Milady," the older man said, looking uneasy. "Has milord called for the horses early?" A look of concern crossed his face.

"No." I noticed he was having lunch on a bale of hay and felt guilty for my intrusion. "Please don't get up. I just wanted to come and see the horses for myself."

"We've got Angus all ready for you, miss," the boy of maybe ten said as he gave the last bucket of grain to a beautiful bay. "Here, over there." He pointed to a large dappled gray warmblood gelding. He was beautiful.

Sensing we were talking about him, Angus stomped his hoof impatiently on the stone floor. As I'd feared, Angus was wearing a beautiful black sidesaddle. For the love of God! I'd never ridden sidesaddle. How the hell would I manage this? I suddenly regretted being so sure of myself when Lord Henry had asked me if I could ride.

A small rush of nerves coursed through my belly at the thought of actually riding again.

Moments later, I was getting used to my new mount Angus. With both my legs facing the same side of the horse I had no idea how to ask him to move forward. I squeezed his side with my left leg, the one that actually rested in the stirrup, and nothing happened. He looked back at me like a mischievous pony. *Sizing me up?*

"For Christ's sake, horse, just go."

I kicked him in the side. He was a little sluggish to respond but at least he started to move. There was a grassy patch next to the stable which he beelined towards, almost unseating me as he pulled the reins out of my hands to have a snack. This was not how I'd imagined my first nineteenth-century ride would play out.

After a small battle of wills, I managed to walk up to the house on horseback, looking more confident than I felt. As I approached, I could see Lord Henry mounting up. He looked over in my direction and smiled. The butler, Phoebus Owens, turned to see what his master was so taken with.

"You are an eager one. Ready to go then, Miss Emma?" Lord Henry called out.

My cheeks were already flushed from the exertion of getting Angus to maintain a normal walk. I could only nod.

He spurred his horse into a trot. Angus immediately woke up and, not wanting to be left behind, picked up the pace right behind Lord Henry's black gelding Dexter. My body bounced along uncomfortably and I struggled to keep my balance. I was determined not to let my discomfort show. Even the jacket, while cute, was already making me sweat and overheat.

How did women do it in this century?

A soft touch on the reins and Angus pulled up easily next to a low-lying tree branch and I removed my coat and flung it over the limb. Lord Henry had continued on and was now quite a distance away. He must not have noticed that we had stopped. Angus was pacing and refused to stand still. He was anxious to catch up with Dexter and I worried he might take off.

My body felt contorted like a pretzel in this saddle. In frustration, I swung my right leg out from the top pommel so that I was sitting astride. This was the only way I knew how to ride. I let Angus have a little rein and asked him to canter. His smooth canter soon turned into a gallop and we were flying through a farmer's field with the afternoon breeze blowing my hair out of its tresses, turning it into a tangled mess. It was exhilarating. It felt wonderful to be back in the saddle. For the first time, I felt in my element. All of my current stresses were on hold and the only thing that mattered was this moment.

We thundered right past Lord Henry, spooking Dexter. Within seconds they were on our tail and I couldn't stop from laughing out loud. Twenty strides ahead I could see a three-foot hedge, no doubt marking the edge of some farmer's field. All I wanted to do was jump it. I had only one stirrup but as long as I kept centered I would be fine. Instinct took over and I started counting my strides and steadying Angus' pace. Realizing I needed to move him up to get the perfect distance, I dug my heels into his side and with the smallest of hesitation and a few clucks from me he left the ground and sailed over the hedge. We pulled up a few strides later and I gave Angus a pat on his neck.

"What a good boy!" I cooed at him, feeling proud that I could still do it.

On the other side of the hedge, Lord Henry looked gobsmacked as he pulled up.

"Miss Emma, are you quite all right? I've never seen Angus jump. It was splendid." Lord Henry broke into a canter and jumped the lower end of the hedge and joined us. "I must admit I was quite worried when I saw you head straight for the thicket," he said, pulling up next to us. "You never told me you were so accomplished."

"Thank you. It all just seemed to come back to me. I guess it's just like riding a bike," I said, still pleased with myself.

"I'm not particularly clear on your meaning. Could you be referring to a velocipede?" His face was flushed and he pulled a small flask from the inside of his jacket, took a sip and held it out to me.

"Yes, exactly, it's something like that," I said and reached out to take the flask. Looking to quench my thirst, I took a larger gulp than I should have and was met with the burning sensation of whiskey. It sent me into a coughing fit.

"Generally it's more palatable if you sip it." Lord Henry laughed.

"Yeah..." I coughed again. "I kinda got that." Handing back the flask, I noticed the White Hart pub in the distance. Riding through the fields, I had lost my sense of direction. It looked different of course without the parking lot and beer garden off the side, but everything else was just the same.

"It's not much farther. Are you all right to continue?" he asked, noticing where I was looking.

"Yes, but"— I hesitated for a moment—"do you think we can pop in afterwards?" I nodded towards the White Hart.

"Finally a woman who can read my mind." He smiled and kicked his horse into a trot. Something about the way he said it gave me a little flip in the belly. Maybe it was how he referred to me as a woman when I'd always thought of myself as a girl. Even at twenty-four, while I was technically a woman, being one and feeling like one were two different things.

Chapter 8

The Greaslys

Our thorough search of the accident site turned up nothing. My purse, it seemed, had not made the journey with me.

This stretch of road looked like any other along these parts. I had wondered if there was some sort of wormhole hidden in the trees and bushes which flanked either side. Would I see the blurred outline of a translucent doorway that would whisk me back to the future? But no matter how many times I walked the area, nothing magical or strange happened. So how did it work then?

Of course Henry was hoping that I might remember what I was doing there and perhaps where I'd come from. Both of those things I knew but couldn't tell him without risking being locked up in some sort of nineteenth-century insane asylum. No matter how many times I played things over in my head there was no logical explanation for how anything had happened. Where did one even begin to look for answers to the illogical?

For now I would settle for a pint at the pub. The White Hart was a welcome sight. I didn't even care that a few eyebrows were raised by my order. Wine or spirits were the usual preference of a woman, I was told by the barman.

Thick smoke filled the air, diffusing the bright sunlight as it reached long rays through the windows. Sweet smells from men's pipes mingled with the delicious aromas of cooking meat. The low-beamed ceiling was exactly how I'd remembered it but the bar itself had yet to experience its twenty-first-century makeover.

A wall divided the place into sections. One was reserved for drinking only, while the other half was more of a dining room where couples enjoyed some old-fashioned pub fare and ale. A staircase off to the far side near the door led to a second story with rooms to rent. Small booths along one wall gave way to sturdy-looking wood tables and chairs. Lord Henry walked over to our table holding two pints of amber ale. *What a déjà vu,* I thought, once again feeling a stab at the thought of Ben.

"My father returns tomorrow from London. Perhaps he can send some letters to his acquaintances to see if anyone may have knowledge of your family." He looked at me with concern. "I am sorry, Miss Emma, I'd hoped that something here might stir your memory. Perhaps tomorrow I should take you into Oxwich, as you may have come through there by train or coach. Someone is bound to have crossed your path." He ran his hand through his thick dark hair.

Sitting across from Lord Henry, I was close enough to notice just how handsome he was. When he turned his gaze on me, I felt the effect of his piercing blue eyes. It left me frozen and speechless. How could anyone even concentrate in his presence?

Despite the length of his sideburns, which he kept neatly trimmed, he was clean-shaven. Although with his complexion, by midday he'd be battling an afternoon shadow. I wondered if he was oblivious to his good looks.

"Thanks for everything you've done," I said, taking another sip of my beer and tearing my eyes away from him, hoping that a cold drink might calm the heat in my cheeks. The taste was more bitter than I was used to, but much better than the whiskey. "I don't want to put you out too much."

"Not at all, Miss Emma. I imagine we'll have you home by tomorrow's eve."

A strained smile crossed my lips. I couldn't depend on Lord Henry's hospitality forever but I had nowhere else to go.

A large middle-aged woman, possibly the owner's wife, brought over two plates of food. One was a dark-looking stew of some sort and the other looked to be a small roast chicken with potatoes and carrots. Placing them on the table, she looked at Lord Henry. "Please let me know if I can bring you anything else, milord." She bowed and curtsied.

"Thank you, Mrs. Greasly." He nodded politely while adjusting a clean white linen across his lap.

Where did I know that name from? It was an unusual name and not a particularly nice one.

"Is the earl returned then from his summer in London?" She gave a not-so-subtle look in my direction, perhaps trying to figure out who I was.

"Not presently, I'm afraid, but he is to return by tomorrow's eve." Lord Henry gave a tight smile and was just about to go back to his beer.

"My Sarah has just returned herself from London," she said, gesturing toward a chubby blonde girl of about twenty-five who was folding napkins over in the corner of the bar. "It has done her a world of good and we're hoping that soon she may have an offer of marriage. She is beautiful, do you not think?"

This woman reminded me of Mrs. Bennet from *Pride and Prejudice*. I had to bite the inside of my cheek to avoid laughing out loud.

“Very, Mrs. Greasly, and I’ve no doubt she will make a most agreeable partner to some lucky chap.” He cleared his throat and gestured towards me. “This is Miss Emma. She’ll be staying at Dormer House for a while. Please give Richard my kind regards,” he said, this time more dismissively.

Of course! A sick feeling engulfed me as I put the pieces together. Her husband was the pub owner Richard Greasly, the one who had found—or should I say would find—Lord Henry’s body after his accident. With a feeling of utter doom, I looked at Lord Henry, who was completely unaware of his own impending demise. He’d already turned his attention to the food.

Satisfied and with the smallest of curtsies to me, Mrs. Greasly went on her way.

“I took the liberty of ordering some food,” he said, already rearranging the plates. “Stew or pheasant?” He looked up at me.

My stomach was growling and the beer had left me a little weak in the knees. However, right now I could hardly think of eating. For a split second, I actually considered telling him what I knew: that he would die very soon, in a horrible way, only steps from this pub. *That’s ridiculous.* How did you even start that conversation? No, he would definitely think I was nuts. I’d have to figure something else out.

“Miss Emma? Are you all right?”

Nothing is all right, I wanted to blurt out.

“Yes, fine,” I lied instead. “Stew, please, although I don’t think I’ve ever tried pheasant.” The smell of food left me mildly rejuvenated.

“It has something of the flavor of both poultry and venison.” He waited for me to start eating before picking up his silverware.

I hadn’t realized how ravenous I actually was until my first bite. It was without a doubt the most delicious stew I’d ever tasted. The meat fell apart in my mouth.

"Do people always try to pawn off their daughters on you like that?" I asked, still amazed at Mrs. Greasly's boldness.

Lord Henry almost choked on his pheasant. "Pawn off?" He laughed. "What on earth do you mean?"

"You know, to get rid of," I said, and he laughed out loud.

"I know what it means, I've just never heard it used in such a way." He recovered and was readjusting the napkin on his lap.

"Oh!"

"I would be lying if I were to say that it has never happened, but Mrs. Greasly is known for trying to 'pawn off', as you say, her daughters on any unmarried man who walks through that door, no matter his position."

"Poor girls. I couldn't imagine having a mother like that." I felt a small tug at my heart. Maybe having a mother like that was better than having no mother at all.

Sarah Greasly was just finishing folding a mountain of napkins and looked our way. She smiled weakly, as if we knew her shame.

"Well, not poor, really." Lord Henry was still continuing the conversation. "For the three other daughters her tactics have worked and they are advantageously wed to wealthy tradesmen. Clearly Mrs. Greasly is on to something." We both laughed. "Not everyone is lucky enough to have a mother so devoted to their children's happiness."

"Do you not have a good relationship with your mother?" I was used to cutting to the chase, but realized too late that I might be prying. Lord Henry seemed taken back by my question. A flicker of sadness—or was it longing?—crossed his expression.

"My mother died when I was very young, but I am told that she was very beautiful. The only other mother I've known is my father's second wife, who's never cared much for me, nor I for her."

"I'm sorry to hear that." I wondered how she'd died. Had he lost her quickly, as I had lost my own mother, with no time to prepare himself for the blow? "Do you look like her? I mean your mother?"

"So I'm told." He looked pensive. Clearly he did not intend to elaborate. "Would you like to try some pheasant?"

Before he could carve off a piece, I took a bite right off his plate as I'd done so many times out of habit with Ben. He looked momentarily mortified, as did all the other pub patrons, but he smiled and asked if he could try the stew. Soon we were eating off each other's plates. He completely ignored the stares we were getting throughout our meal, but I couldn't help but feel a bit self-conscious. In the future I would probably need to address my table manners if I was to blend in and not attract too much negative attention.

We returned to the house side by side on horseback. The whole time he gave me the rundown of the area, who lived nearby and a few fun bits of gossip. It felt already like we were old friends. He was different outside the walls of his home, where there was such formality. Here he was just like any other man of his age trying to find his place in the world, so oblivious to the fate that awaited him.

The knowledge of what was to come weighed heavily on my heart. For the first time my own problems paled by comparison.

Chapter 9

A Birth

By the time we reached Dormer House the sun was low on the horizon. No one came out to greet us, so we brought the horses into the stable and untacked. There was an apple left on a hay bale, so I scooped it up and gave half to Angus. The other half I fed to Dexter, who almost swallowed my fingers along with it.

A horse grunted in the stall next door and I stuck my head in to check on the mare. She was lying down looking uncomfortable. Her back legs seemed stiff and she kept looking towards her belly anxiously.

"Lord Henry?" I called after him.

He came out of the tack room holding my jacket. "What is it?" He brushed the bits of straw from my jacket before handing it to me.

"This mare, she looks like she may have colic." Having dealt with this before with one of my own horses, I knew how serious it could be even in my time. It was a gastrointestinal condition that was the leading cause of premature death in horses. Often it meant a trip to the veterinary hospital and surgery.

"Oh?" He looked at the mare in question with concern. Entering her stall, he spoke softly to keep her calm. "I don't think that's her problem." He looked amused. "I think Betsy is in foal."

"She's having her baby now? Should we get some help?" My heart started to beat a little faster. Excitement burst through me. In all my years around horses I'd never been in the right place at the right time to be part of this.

"No, there isn't time. I can see one hoof and maybe a muzzle already sticking out." He gestured to the far side of the stable while taking off his jacket and rolling up his sleeves. "Would you pass me some fresh linens from the tack room and one of those knives the grooms keep with the tools over in that grooming box by the corner?"

"Yes, of course." Excited at the prospect of witnessing my first live birth, I could feel the adrenaline coursing through my body, making my limbs feel numb and awkward. I laid the items next to the stall door and hovered just behind Lord Henry's right shoulder.

"What do we do now?" I asked, eager to help in the process.

"Nothing really, it won't be long now," he said. "Is this the first time you've seen this?"

"Yes, in person that is. I've seen it on YouTube before but never…" He looked confused. I realized my slip. "I mean in books… you know, drawings… it's like a book series kind of thing. It's an American thing." He nodded and I continued more carefully. "I've always wanted to see it for myself."

"*You Tube*? Is that some kind of medical journal?" he asked, looking genuinely interested. "I'm not familiar with it."

"Um, something like that, I suppose you could say. There are probably… lots of medical references… there." *Nerves.* I willed myself to stop talking. "Oh, look!" Happy to redirect his attention, I pointed towards the mare, who had just managed to get the foal's entire head out but seemed to be straining.

A look of trepidation crossed his face.

"It looks like the foal's shoulder may be caught. I see only one hoof not two." He bent down towards the mare's tail, reached his hands inside and felt around. "I can scarcely feel the foal's leg. It's a little twisted but my hand is too big to right it…" His eyes locked on to mine with genuine concern. The mare grunted and shifted her body to help with the discomfort.

"Should I try?" I was already walking over to join him next to the mare.

She watched me anxiously. Her breathing was quick and strained. The poor thing was in a lot of pain and I was sure the two of us poking and prodding wasn't helping. Lord Henry moved over to give me space. I rolled the sleeve of my blouse all the way up my arm. Just as I started sliding my hand inside Betsy, I felt his hand on my arm guiding me to the foal's shoulder.

As horrific as this was, I didn't feel the least bit squeamish. It was the close proximity to Lord Henry that I found the most unnerving. Over the musty smell of sweat, there was a touch of lavender from his freshly laundered shirt, which mingled nicely with a hint of alcohol from our afternoon beer. Ever since dating Ben I had never been this close to another man. My belly stirred and the hairs on the back of my neck stood at attention. My inner temperature spiked considerably.

"Do you feel it?" he whispered.

Guilt flooded all my senses and snapped me back to the job at hand.

There is definitely something wrong with me.

"Yes, I think, but what should I do?"

"Reach down towards the knee and gently tug it upwards."

It was slippery, making it hard to get a firm hold, but I tugged and felt a small pop.

"Shit!" I blurted before I could stop myself. "My God, I think I broke its leg." I was horrified that I'd damaged the tiny foal for life.

Tears welled up in my eyes.

"Nonsense, it's fine. If you felt a pop, that was the joint going back in." His voice was calm and slightly amused. "They are incredibly flexible at this age, I assure you."

I gave another small tug and the leg moved towards me. The mare grunted again, straining her body to push the foal out. With one more giant heave the baby came flooding out, still in its sac.

Warm liquid poured onto my skirt and I reached for the linens that Lord Henry was already handing me.

Leaning across me, he carefully cut the sac near the foal's face with the knife and pulled the tissue back, helping to free the tiny creature. Half in my lap, the baby looked up with glossy eyes, no doubt exhausted from its journey. Tears streamed down my face. What a powerful feeling to hold life or death in my own hands and see life prevail. I felt proud of myself for delivering a foal.

"Well done, Miss Emma," Lord Henry said, chuckling.

He noticed my face and became more serious. His hand was in mine without warning, giving me a tingling feeling that shot straight up my arm as he helped me to my feet. With his other hand he passed me a handkerchief from his pocket which I used to wipe my face. Overcome with emotion, I could barely do more than smile until I became aware of how wet and filthy I'd become.

"Miss Barnsby is going to have a cow." I hadn't meant to say it out loud. I looked to Lord Henry apologetically but he was unable to move, he was laughing so hard.

"I don't think I've ever heard a lady speak as you do." It was his turn to wipe away the tears now.

"So I've been told," I said, and raised my hands in surrender. "How did you know what to do?" Suddenly, I saw Lord Henry in a whole new light. How could a man in his position know how to mend arms and deliver foals? I had always pictured lords and ladies of these grand homes to be much too important to get their hands dirty.

"I've always had an interest in the ways things work, so I've spent a great deal of time figuring it out." He was trying to be humble. I could see my sudden interest in his abilities made him uncomfortable. Shy even. A contrast to his usual confident demeanor. Did he not feel worthy of praise? Or was he simply not used to getting any?

Betsy was bonding with her baby, licking the rest of the sac from its furry coat. We stepped out of her stall and left them to it. Crisis averted, we started to head up the path towards the house silently, both of us digesting what we had just participated in.

It was only when we got close to the house that I noticed that something was different. There was far more activity than earlier in the day. Servants I didn't recognize were rushing about bringing trunks and luggage from a black carriage. The two-horse team nibbled on hay from a net attached to their bridles, oblivious to the chaos around them. The carriage driver, a small weasel-like man, watched us with squinty eyes as we approached. From what Lord Henry had explained, they usually took the train in to Oxwich and had their driver pick them up there. I wondered whether this was the same man who had driven the carriage that had apparently struck me.

Lord Henry put his coat back on and tried to smooth his hair, which had not seemed the least bit out of place. He looked down to me, his expression withdrawn and crisp. Amazed by the transformation that had taken place in seconds right before my eyes, I watched him carefully. He was no longer the same man I'd just spent the afternoon with. This man was now in character.

"Are you ready to meet the Earl of Pembrooke?" Lord Henry said without even a hint of a smile.

This sounded ominous. *Do I have a choice?* A hot bath first didn't seem to be an option. The lump was back in my throat, making it hard to speak. How could anyone who had raised such a son be all that bad?

Just as we came up the few stairs I felt a small tug on my hair and realized that Lord Henry had removed a stray piece of straw that had been tangled in the mess.

Chapter 10

The Earl

Phoebus, the butler, opened the door. His usual stoic expression registered a certain amount of shock as he took in our appearances—mostly mine, I was sure. Just as quickly, he recovered and bowed towards Lord Henry.

"Lord Henry, your father is in the library at the moment," he said, giving me a sideways glance.

"Thank you, Phoebus," Lord Henry said as he breezed straight past the man. "Let McCleary know Betsy's had her foal." Phoebus nodded like he'd been given instructions for a meat roast. How could anyone not be moved or the least bit excited by the news?

Unsure what to do, I simply followed Lord Henry straight into the library.

"Ah, there you are, Henry. What kind of mischief have you been up to this time?" the earl said by way of greeting when we walked into the room.

What kind of hello was that? He hadn't quite noticed me at first but even when he did he paid little attention. He looked nothing like Lord Henry. He was easily half a foot shorter and significantly wider. Perhaps a life of indulgence. His fine tailored clothes bulged ever so slightly as he paced by the unlit fireplace. Heavily salted mutton-chop whiskers flanked his face.

"Good evening to you too, Father. I trust you had a nice journey from London." Lord Henry didn't wait for a response. "I thought you were due to arrive tomorrow. Why the change of plans?"

"I received some alarming reports that you've gotten yourself into some trouble and thought I should come straight away to help clean up your mess. This is not a good time for rumors and scandal, you know." The earl wasn't able to contain his impatience even in front of strangers.

It was starting to feel awkward, but without the ability to make myself invisible, I pretended to be examining the upholstery.

"May I introduce Miss Emma Clayton." Lord Henry gestured in my direction. "And if by trouble you mean the accident, I have done everything in my power to see that Miss Clayton has received a doctor and hospitality while she recovers." He had been holding his hands in tight fists, but now adjusted his jacket cuffs. Was this a nervous habit?

The earl glanced in my direction. Our eyes met briefly and I gave him a sheepish smile.

"She looks quite recovered to me." He was now looking at his son. It was a strange feeling to be talked about while I was standing right there. This felt like a bad reality TV show unfolding right before my eyes where the audience squirmed with discomfort. The only difference I was unable to change the channel and seemed to be the subject that was causing the issue.

"With a severe blow to her head, she has been unable to remember much. Not only of the accident but where she was staying and who we might contact." Lord Henry was struggling to keep calm.

"How very convenient indeed," muttered the earl under his breath, but loud enough for both of us to hear. "Are you sure this woman is not simply mad?" He gave me another quick onceover like I was a dirty street urchin.

"Oh, please, I'm quite certain," Lord Henry said impatiently. "I've already canvassed the nearby estates in search of anyone who may have a missing person."

Shaking his head, the earl studied me. He ran his tongue along the inside of his lower lip as if he were contemplating his next move. His hand brushed against his whiskers.

"Sir… I mean Lord… umm… Pembrooke." My palms were sweating but I couldn't bear another second of this.

He looked at his son now.

"An American?" He softened a little. Not exactly the reaction I'd been anticipating. Usually Americans were met with contempt but in England during this period I had imagined there was even less tolerance given the few decades since the most recent war of 1812.

"I am so sorry for the inconvenience," I continued. "I would love more than anything to go back home." They had no idea how far that really was or how on earth that could even be accomplished. "Your son—Lord Henry, I mean—has been very kind and I wish to thank you for the hospitality I have been shown here."

Something shifted in the earl. Perhaps I'd surprised him somehow. Lord Henry wore that same expression on occasion when I'd done or said something unexpected.

"Well, Miss Clayton"—his bad temper was slowly dissipating—"I am glad to hear you have been comfortable at Dormer House. We are at your service until you are recovered and your relations found."

I smiled at this, but what was going to happen next? How long did I have before I would overstay my welcome? This man had a very short fuse, it seemed.

"Father, I thought I should take Miss Emma to Oxwich tomorrow to see if she might recognize anything or perhaps someone might know her. She may well have traveled through there at some point." Lord Henry waited patiently while the earl mulled this over.

"Very well, you can take the carriage in with Harris, as he will be going to collect Mama from the train. You will need to ride back though, as there won't be room on the return. Your brother and sister are returning with her." The earl walked away from the fireplace where he had been standing and sat down behind a large mahogany desk which contained unopened letters, blank paper and a selection of quills with ink pots. "I will send out some letters tomorrow and make some more inquiries. Meanwhile, Henry, send for the doctor to drop by in the morning so that I might have a word." With that we were both dismissed as the earl started to pore over a small stack of letters.

We moved out of earshot.

"That went a little better than I expected." Lord Henry was visibly more relaxed.

"Is he always like that?" I wondered out loud.

"Much worse, I'm afraid. You'll think him a lamb compared to my stepmother." The thought made us both shudder. "I am dreadfully sorry for the mess you now find yourself in."

"Don't be. I would never have delivered a foal if it weren't for you."

His eyes brightened and I turned to go to my room. It was time to get out of these clothes and start to make a plan. What was I to do? Invisible hands kept my feet planted in place. Why did I feel so good with this virtual stranger?

"Do you feel up to the journey to Oxwich tomorrow? It may be a long shot, but if it sparks anything it would be worth it." Henry looked hopeful and eager to help. His dark hair had fallen down over his right eye, giving him a mischievous look. Why was he trying so hard to help me? Maybe he was just eager to get rid of me.

"It's worth a shot." I tried to mimic his optimism but I knew this would be another dead end. My heart sank a little with this knowledge. On the bright side, I needed to enjoy as much of this experience as I could because once they realized this was hopeless and I became more of a burden on the family, where would I be then? "Can I ride Angus again?"

"Only if you promise to behave." There was a hint of reprimand in his tone before he smiled. His smile was contagious and I found myself unable to turn away from him and walk up the stairs.

I was starting to wonder if spending more time with Lord Henry was the wisest move. I needed his support while I figured out how to get back to my old life. Without his kindness, I would be out on the street. The more I got to know him though, the more difficult it became to weave this web of lies.

"Ah, umm…" Phoebus the butler had been observing our exchange. "A letter has arrived for you, milord."

"Thank you, Phoebus." He took the letter and opened it right away. It seemed like the perfect time to make a break for my room so I turned and headed up the stairs unnoticed.

"Have McCleary ready my horse, would you, Phoebus?" Out of the corner of my eye I watched Lord Henry walk towards the great room with urgency.

Chapter 11

A Thief

Miss Barnsby was already waiting for me at my door.

"What the devil have you been up to?" she said, waving a hand near her nose. "I hope you haven't gone and ruined your clothes." I floated into the room while she scolded me. "There better not be mending to do."

A bath had already been drawn for me. Just as one would salivate with the smell of food, my body ached with the anticipation of warm water to soothe my sore muscles. Between the accident and the day of riding today, I was a wreck. What I wouldn't do for a Korean spa at this very moment. The thought of 1850's English women naked together, going through the equivalent of a human car wash, made me chuckle.

Miss Barnsby in turn gave me a stern look, indicating I had completely lost my mind. The sun was just starting to set, bathing the walls and furnishings in a rich warm glow. It was my favorite time of day. Everything always looked better in those orange tones.

Lavender and honeysuckle soaked in the water, giving it a subtle, sweet floral scent. Miss Barnsby busied herself with undoing my corset a little more aggressively than was necessary. Had I not needed her help I would have been more than happy to undress myself.

The water did not disappoint. For the first time in what seemed like the longest twenty-four hours of my life my body relaxed. Miss Barnsby finally took her leave after I assured her that I would not drown in the bath and that I would be staying in my room for the night. Now I was finally alone, my mind drifted to Lord Henry and I found myself smiling. When I closed my eyes I pictured him looking at me as he had after we'd delivered the foal and I felt a flutter of excitement in my belly.

Guilt washed over me as I thought of Ben. The man who loved me—my fiancé, no less—was probably worried sick. How would I ever get back? Guilt was quickly replaced with despair and the tears started to flow without warning.

I wasn't sure how long I stayed that way, but when the numbness wore off I realized that the water in the tub was now cold and the sun had set, leaving me with only the silvery light of the moon. My face tingled from the dried tears, which I rinsed before stepping out of the bath. On my bed, Miss Barnsby had laid out a nightie similar to the one I had worn previously, except for the intricate blue flower pattern around the neck. It looked more like a sister-wife outfit from one of those Mormon compounds Utah was famous for. A far cry from the tank-and-boxer-shorts combo I loved to wear. If she could see me now, my friend April would be rolling on the floor. "You have to be kidding me!" she'd say, as she always did when she didn't approve of something.

Once I got dressed, my stomach started to growl. Crying always left me ravenous. When I poked my head out the door, it seemed as if everyone had retired for the night. Most of the oil lamps had been turned off except for a few positioned near the staircase and in the great hall. I tiptoed down the steps in search of something to nibble on.

The large grandfather clock which sat on the staircase landing indicated it was quarter past eleven. Fortunately the dining room was set for tomorrow's breakfast and they'd already put out a bowl of fruit, which sat on the buffet table near some additional glasses and silverware. Taking a napkin off the table, I wrapped an apple, some grapes, an orange and a small sharp knife in a makeshift hobo sack and turned to go back towards the stairs.

"Ah-ha! Stop right there, you thief!" yelled a male voice.

Startled, I nearly dropped my fruit. It was impossible to make out who the booming voice belonged to, as they were standing in the doorway backlit by the only light. At first I had no idea it was directed at me so I looked around the room for the real perpetrator.

"Put down the silver this very instant," he demanded when I didn't move.

"What?" Confusion led to fear as I realized he was in fact talking to me. By now, I could hear movement somewhere in the house followed by footsteps. "What are you talking about?" I stammered. "I was just..."

"Phoebus? What is the meaning of this?" Finally a voice I did recognize. Although I could only make out his silhouette, I recognized his tall lean body.

Phoebus, so convinced that I was about to flee, came rushing towards me, grabbing at my bag.

"This woman is nothing but a common thief!" He succeeded in wrenching the bag out of my hands and as he did the fruit went tumbling free, with the apple rolling all the way to Lord Henry's feet.

Anger. Humiliation. I wasn't sure which I felt more strongly but as I opened my mouth to defend my honor, Lord Henry beat me to it.

"Phoebus, you absolute imbecile! Remove yourself from my sight before I have the police remove you for assaulting this woman."

Phoebus' comb over was disheveled. His long features drooped like a hound dog's in this light. He looked to Lord Henry as a child would after being put on a time-out for bad behavior.

"My deepest apologies, Miss Clayton," Phoebus mumbled behind gritted teeth. Without making eye contact, he bowed to Lord Henry and walked briskly from the room.

Even though he had been an ass, I couldn't help but feel sorry for him. It was humiliating to watch a grown man get in trouble. Especially with someone half his age.

"I cannot convey to you how desperately sorry I am for my servant's behavior." Henry was already stooping down to pick up some of the discarded fruit.

"You know, I was sort of skulking around foraging for food. Don't be too hard on Phoebus. He was just defending your property from a stranger, even though he did sort of scare the shiii… I mean… pants off me."

I was still shaken by the ordeal. It had all happened so quickly. The grapes were smushed into the carpet and I bent down in an effort to pick them out as much as I could.

"We've had some difficulty with thievery of late, I'm afraid, and Phoebus has taken it upon himself to act as watchdog." He was holding my apple and a squashed orange in one large hand. "Are you hungry then? Shall I ring for something?"

"Oh, hell, no. I don't want anyone else waking up for me." When I stood up Lord Henry quickly averted his eyes as he noticed for the first time that I was in a nightie. "I would settle for a glass of wine, though, if that's not too much trouble."

Before I'd even finished, Lord Henry had wriggled out of his own jacket and was putting it over my shoulders. His concern over my modesty was sweet and my body responded to the heat of his jacket and the smell of him all over it.

"I think we could both use one." He took the grape carnage from my hand and with his hand gently on my back guided me through the great hall into the 'great parlor', the name I remembered from the tour. It was the largest and most public of the rooms but used primarily as a family sitting room.

A coal fire was burning on the other side, giving it a smoky, sulfury smell. Pulling Lord Henry's jacket tighter around my shoulders, I collapsed into a hard, uncomfortable armchair and tucked my feet up under me.

When he returned with two glasses of red wine he glanced only momentarily at the way I was sitting. Okay, maybe it wasn't so ladylike, but I couldn't be bothered to move. The wine smelled delicious, with a hint of blackberries. I had to make an effort not to down the whole thing in one go.

"So tell me about this 'thieving'. That is, if you don't mind."

He waved it off. "Not much to it, really. It's quite normal in a house this size that the odd thing goes on a walkabout. Phoebus just takes it very personally, as it is the butler's job to lock the valuables up every night." Lord Henry looked tired.

"Oh, you think that things were just misplaced then? Is that why he's always hovering around in corners?" In the last day I'd been up and around the house, I often walked into rooms completely unaware that the butler was standing somewhere until I got up to leave and there he was like a statue. *Very creepy.*

"Well, as head of all the staff he does carry a great deal of weight on his shoulders, I suppose, and he certainly keeps an eye on the carryings-on throughout the house. He's been with the family for a long time so he's gotten quite good at skulking around." Henry laughed at this. He too had noticed how creepy the guy was. "As for the things that have gone missing, they are really just trivial things that could have dropped on the floor over dinner or been knocked under tables. I've misplaced cufflinks and pocket watches before and I've only got myself to worry about." There was a hint of heaviness in the tone of his voice when he said this last bit, but I could have misinterpreted.

"Are you happy with your life?" I wasn't sure what possessed me to ask this, but I had gotten so used to asking myself this question lately that it flew out before I could even censor it.

There was a very heavy silence and I started to wonder if maybe I had overstepped my bounds. I chugged the last of my wine, not knowing what else to do and unsure where to look.

"That's a very odd question, Miss Emma."

Okay, here it comes. He's going to tell me how inappropriate I am.

"Not one person has ever asked me that. Am I happy with my life? Well, most would consider me fortunate. I have wealth and a title but what does that really all mean? I am bound by those obligations. The idea of following my heart and pursuing what I love is forbidden to me, so tell me, what happiness could there truly be left for me? No"—he shook his head—"I'm afraid it is a luxury a man in my position isn't afforded—so I don't even entertain it."

Not quite the answer I was anticipating. Lord Henry was looking to me for answers now. I had opened a Pandora's box without realizing.

"That's just crazy! Why couldn't you be an earl and do the things you enjoy? You love to heal, don't you? Watching you with that mare, you just seemed to have an incredible instinct. And what about the way you took care of my injuries?" I held my arm up to prove a point. "Most people struggle their whole lives looking for things they're good at."

"A nobleman with a trade? My father forbids it. I am to follow in his footsteps in politics, the only thing suitable for an earl." He spat this last bit out with contempt.

My heart broke for him. We had opposite problems. He knew exactly what he wanted but couldn't have it and I had all the options but couldn't settle on any one thing. We were both paralyzed. His passion was inspiring though, if I could even just have a thimbleful.

"Couldn't you just talk to your dad… I mean, the earl? Make him understand?"

He had grabbed the bottle of wine and was now refilling my glass.

"Ha. You have met my father? He would disown me and I would be turned out with nothing and no means." Lord Henry drained half his glass in one gulp. My legs were already feeling the effects of the wine as it navigated through the rest of my body. A dull painkiller and a welcome one.

"Practicing medicine is a very acceptable career. You're good at it, Henry."

He looked at me when I said his name.

"Maybe you should just follow your heart and screw everybody else. What is all the wealth in the world without happiness?" That last bit sounded like a Hallmark card. Now I was making myself gag.

"Spoken by someone with nothing."

That stung. Until he'd said that I hadn't realized how truly alone I really was. I knew it was the wine and his frustration talking, but I could feel myself withdraw.

"That was unkind. I apologize."

"Don't worry, you're right. I have no business talking about things I can't possibly understand." I made a move to get up. My ego was bruised and all I wanted to do was shut myself back in my room. "I'm exhausted. If you don't mind, I'm going to bed." Reluctantly, I removed his jacket and gave it back to him, not caring how revealing my nightie might or might not be.

"I never meant to insult you. Please stay."

"It's late and if we're going to Oxwich tomorrow I should get some rest." The bottle of wine on the side table was half full. I picked it up. "May I?" And without waiting for a response I took it with me. Although I didn't look back, I could feel his eyes on my back as I made my way out the door and up the stairs to my room.

The smell of lavender still permeated the air when I walked through the door to my room. A dirty ring had formed around the bath from the water left there. I hated leaving things on such a bad note with Lord Henry, but I didn't feel up to facing the reality his statement evoked. It was true. I was someone with nothing. All the more reason I had to figure out a way back to my time. If I'd gotten here, there had to be a way back. Maybe tomorrow would bring answers.

In my haste to make a graceful exit I had left my glass behind, so now I took small swigs of wine right from the bottle, like a proper wino. When I was a young teenager riding horses I used to get dropped off at the barn for the day. One of the grooms there, Willy, who was actually a middle-aged woman, used to drive me to grab our lunch. She always drove with a bottle of wine in a brown paper bag wedged between her thighs. Every time she would take a sip the car would swerve slightly into the oncoming traffic lane. Never enough that I was worried we'd crash but just enough that my hand would make a move to grab the steering wheel. I said a mental cheers to Willy now as I took another sip.

When I had settled myself comfortably in bed with the wine close at hand on the side table, I noticed a note had been slid under the door. Had I walked over it when I'd come in or had it been put through more recently? Impossible to tell. Maybe Henry felt he needed to apologize. I peeled back the many layers of bedcovers and picked up the folded sheet of paper.

In a childlike scrawl it read, *I am on to you.*

Icy fingers crept up my spine and the soothing effects of the wine instantly dissipated.

Chapter 12

Wildflowers

Despite all the wine I scarcely slept a wink. My mind turned over and over the meaning of the note and who could have put it under my door. Every time I heard a creak in the house my imagination set off a flurry of new worries.

My exhaustion must have kicked in sometime after the sky turned that pale gray just before the sun came up. A knock at the door startled me and I came to with my face stuck to my pillow in a pile of drool. Attractive.

Before I could even respond, Miss Barnsby walked through my room clucking her disapproval. Shuffling about like a woman on a mission, she set about putting out my clothes and opening the windows to let in some fresh air. She didn't even try to mask her contempt for her job this morning.

"The doctor will be up in a minute to check on you and then you'll be leaving for Oxwich with Lord Henry." She filled the pitcher of water on the dresser, laid out a small bowl of apples and then turned back to me. "Come on then, up with ye, his lordship wants you presentable and I think I've got me work cut out tis mornin'." While she spoke she arranged something on my dresser. "I'm not sure why Lord Henry asked me to put these poor wee things in here, but he thought you might like them," she mumbled under her breath.

My eyes cracked open and I saw the small vase of wildflowers Miss Barnsby was moaning on about. I got out of bed and walked over to the dresser. Ignoring Miss Barnsby's questioning looks, I bent my head to smell them.

"I love them." How had he known? He must have felt bad for last night.

The flowers definitely lifted my spirits. I had wallowed in my own self-pity for long enough and it was time I took matters into my own hands.

Once I was appropriately primped and corseted, I sat in the chair by the window awaiting the doctor. Miss Barnsby, satisfied with her efforts, left in a cloud of petticoats and undergarments.

Other than Lord Henry, most of the men I had met in this time were quite short. Dr. Bainbridge was no exception. His dark suit was snug around his rotund torso. No stranger to rich foods, I suspected. Heavily in need of a trim, his sideburns were wild and unkempt. Perched on the end of his nose were small wire glasses. When he stood too close I could hear a slight wheezing to his every breath, not a trait that instilled huge amounts of confidence in someone in his line of work. How anyone could take him seriously was beyond me.

"Have any of your memories of the events leading up to the accident come back to you yet? Anything at all, even the smallest thing?" he asked while cleaning his glasses with a handkerchief.

"All I remember is waking up in this bed." I lied easily.

"Have you awoken disorientated since that time?" He was now examining the back of my head where I'd hit it. It was still tender where he touched it.

"Not since then." Contrary to Lord Henry's touch, this man's made my skin crawl.

"The earl tells me you are from America. Do you remember the boat ride over here?" He was now searching my eyes, most likely looking at my pupils.

"No, none of it." Which wasn't a lie, as I'd taken a plane over, not a boat, but that was not a detail I wanted to elaborate on. I'd even upgraded at the last moment for extra leg room. Love the extra leg room.

"What about your childhood?" Okay, now he was entering dangerous territory. "Do you remember much of that?"

"Only snippets, the odd bit." I thought it was better to avoid all of that. He squinted as if he was putting the pieces together.

"But you remembered your name?" He was getting ready to finish, I hoped.

"Yes, that's true. I always knew my name." Now I was wondering where he was going with this.

"Remarkable," he said to no one in particular.

"Is that common? To forget everything except your name?" The best tactic was sometimes to redirect the questioning.

"Common? No. But it has been known to happen. In most cases, Miss Clayton, the patient will slowly regain more and more memories as the days go on and in some cases a patient may wake up in the morning and remember everything. I suspect that in your case, things will start coming back to you by the end of the week." He smiled at this and gave me a pat of encouragement on the leg. Throughout his examination he'd stood much too close and I felt my personal space was being violated. He looked at me now with a lecherous grin that made me uneasy.

When the door to my room opened and Lord Henry stood there I finally let out the breath I hadn't realized I'd been holding. It was as if he'd read my mind.

"Dr. Bainbridge?" he said, with an amused look on his face. "My father waits for your consultation in his study. If you are through here"—he looked to me with one raised brow, and then settled once again on the doctor—"I would be happy to escort you."

"Very well," Dr. Bainbridge wheezed.

While the doctor gathered his things at a snail's pace, I mouthed the words 'thank you' to Lord Henry, who smiled and bowed his head in acknowledgment. Perhaps also in apology for last night. As far as that went, it was already forgotten.

Once alone, I adjusted the hat I was meant to wear and took the gloves for my ride home later. Miss Barnsby had left a few apples this morning so I grabbed those for my trusty steed Angus and made my way downstairs. Lord Henry was waiting by the door in his riding clothes with his top hat in hand. He offered me his arm, which I took gratefully, acknowledging that all was well between us again, and we headed out the front door.

I was anxious to be out of that house away from the earl, Miss Barnsby, Phoebus and now even Dr. Bainbridge. Harris, the coach driver, looked me up and down as I stepped up into the carriage, but I hardly paid any attention. Our horses, Angus and Dexter, were tied to the back of the covered coach and would be coming with us on our journey. When we were settled and the coach was off, Lord Henry brought out a small picnic from a basket he had tucked under his seat.

"I knew we wouldn't have much of a chance to eat this morning, so I brought a few things in case you were hungry." In his basket he had boiled eggs, cheese, bread and fruit.

"Great, because I am starving. Thanks for the flowers by the way."

He shrugged like it was nothing.

My mouth salivated and I dove in. Riding in a coach was a lot like those hay rides I used to go on as a kid when we'd visit the local farms. It was a bumpy ride without shock absorbers, so after five minutes everyone was pretty much over it. Now those memories came flooding back as I tried eating with chattering teeth. It felt like my fillings were going to get knocked right out of my mouth and after only a few nibbles of bread and cheese I pretty much gave up.

"How long until we get there?" Five minutes in I was desperate to know how much longer I'd have to stand this for.

"Only an hour less a quarter," he said as if this was a good thing.

"Oh," was about all the enthusiasm I could muster. My backside was already feeling numb from the continuous thumping. The other thing that I hadn't accounted for was the lack of windows. They had opted for the covered coach as the skies were cloudy and threatening rain. While there were small windows on either side, there were none in the front or back. So it wasn't long before I started to feel car-sick, or should I say coach-sick.

Poor Lord Henry watched in horror as I turned white. By pure stubbornness of will I managed to get all the way to Oxwich with only one stop to throw up. The rest of the trip Lord Henry watched me carefully for any sign I was about to lose it. I wasn't sure who was more tense throughout the journey. It wasn't exactly the trip either of us had bargained for.

Once there I struggled to recover any dignity I had left. He was kind enough to take me to a charming little tea house so that I could freshen up and we could enjoy a hot cup of tea and settle our nerves.

"I'm glad that's over with," I said, relieved to regain feeling in my bum.

"Ha. I gather you've not traveled a great deal by coach?" Now that he was no longer worried for me his sense of humor had returned.

"Apparently not. I can't stand not seeing where I'm going. I've always had a touch of motion sickness. That's why I could never read in the car… coach." I recovered quickly.

"You must have been a real pleasure on the boat over here." He laughed.

"Haha… I'm glad my misery is entertaining." I thought of my comfortable plane ride to Heathrow: champagne and movies. He smiled at me and finished his tea.

"We should make our way to the train station and the two inns in town. I have some business to attend first, so I thought you might want to look at a few shops."

It was nice to be in a small town for a change. Oxwich as I knew it in the future was still a small town, but significantly larger than it was now. However, the main square was almost the same. Instead of cars there were horse carriages plodding along the cobbled streets. The foot traffic was the same with the square in the center of the town acting as farmers' market and craft fair—livestock being sold here and there, pigs, chickens, and goats with the odd horse or cow. The shops bordering the market ranged from book shops, dressmakers, coffee houses to bakeries and butchers. A little apothecary sold all kinds of lotions and potions for this or that ailment. Small boys of maybe six sold local papers at every corner. The crowd did not look as sophisticated as you might picture in London at this time, but everyone was well dressed, if their clothes were a bit on the simpler side.

One of the most glaring differences was the smell. It smelled like shit of every kind and lots of it. I noticed a man on the far side of the square whose job it seemed to be to deal with the mountains of it. Equipped with a small wheelbarrow and shovel, he hardly seemed to make a dent.

Lord Henry checked his pocket watch.

"I am fine to walk around if you have somewhere you need to be." I could tell that he was uncomfortable leaving me in the middle of the chaos.

"Are you sure you don't want an escort? I could have Harris accompany…"

"Oh, please, no!" I interrupted him. There was no way I wanted to be anywhere near that weird little man. He gave me the creeps. "I'll be fine. I noticed a book shop in the square that I'd love to check out."

He laughed at how quickly I'd rejected his idea of an escort. "Very well, Miss Clayton. I will only be about a half hour. I shall come looking for you there." He handed me a small pouch of coins. "In case you find something you like."

"Oh, I can't take this." I was instantly uncomfortable taking any kind of a handout. I'd always had my own money. Even with Ben I'd always split the bills right down the middle.

"I insist." His hands cupped over mine so that I couldn't hand back the money. The feeling of electricity coursed through my entire body. I almost felt the need to withdraw because of its intensity. Lord Henry held my eyes for just a second longer before both of us pulled away.

"Take care Miss Emma, I will be no more than a quarter hour," he said simply and turned to walk away.

Chapter 13

Down the Rabbit Hole

The book store was probably the tiniest little shop I'd ever set foot in. Shelves extended all the way up to the ceiling, which was high, and a ladder was needed to reach many of the books that cluttered every space. Most of the books were used but some of the newer additions were located on the lower shelves. A young boy of maybe ten with a wiry little frame was up and down the rickety old ladder several times to retrieve whatever was needed. An older, stout man of maybe fifty called orders to him from the ground. He seemed to be the one who knew where everything lived.

"What can I do you for, miss?" The older gentleman had kind eyes and was eager to help.

"Do you have any John Keats?

"Well, let me see, I believe I have some Keats. You know he's quite popular these days and his books don't stay in my shop for long." He cleaned his spectacles with his shirt sleeve and set about his search as he spoke. "Would *The Eve of St. Agnes* be of interest? It's a used copy but beautifully preserved."

"Anything you have would be great," I said, looking in wonder at all the old treasures the old man had on the shelves. "Do you happen to have *Jane Eyre* by Currer Bell?" Charlotte Brontë's book had first been published under a pen name in an attempt to mask her gender.

I wasn't sure how much money Lord Henry had given me but I was pretty sure it would more than cover it.

He made a tsking sound with his mouth.

"*Jane Eyre* has caused quite a stir, by and by I'm not sure all the fuss is warranted. If you ask me, I find the writing a bit coarse. I do have one copy however if you're still keen on it."

"Yes, I am keen on it." Speculation that Currer Bell was a woman had not only contributed to its popularity but also its criticism.

A beautiful hand-drawn book called *Human Anatomy* caught my eye.

"Oh, and what about that one?"

"That one is dear. Is that for your own use?" He eyed me up and down.

Was it scandalous for a woman to buy a book with pictures of the human body, I wondered?

"For a friend." Lord Henry would love it. I couldn't wait to show him.

The old man called out to his assistant and the boy quickly retrieved the books in question.

"That will be two sovereigns"—he paused to made the mental calculation—"and three bob, miss." The man walked behind a small desk, getting ready to take care of the financial part of our transaction. "Would you be putting that on account?" He once again cleaned his spectacles and started rifling through some papers.

"No, I'll pay now." The money purse Lord Henry had given me felt heavy with coins but I really had no idea how much was in there and in what denominations. There was a moment where I feared looking like an idiot, but rather than let that panic take root I opened the purse and rummaged through until I came up with two gold coins, a few silver and some copper ones. Unsure what the sovereigns or even bobs looked like, I handed over all the coins in my hand. The shop owner took the two gold coins, three silver florins and gave me back the rest.

"Thank you, miss. I'll have Alfred wrap those. Would you like to return later to pick them up?"

The idea of schlepping that big heavy book around for the day was not appealing. "Can I come back after lunch?" I asked, dropping the extra coins back in my tiny change purse.

"We will have your package waiting for you then. What name can I put on it?" He was grinning ear to ear.

"Emma. Emma Clayton." Feeling rather pleased with myself for my first nineteenth-century purchase, I decided to continue on my shopping spree.

When I came out I looked around for the apothecary. I'd only ever read about them. They were the pharmacies of the past. I hopped over piles of horse manure as I made my way across the square to the store, which sat on the corner opposite a tea shop.

Inside, the contrast to the book store was overwhelming. Here everything was neatly in its place. Minimalist. Large glass bottles lined long wooden shelves behind the counter. Much smaller ones were grouped on small tables and clearly labeled. While the shop seemed sparse by comparison, it had a large selection of everything from hair tonics to poultices for scrapes and cuts. There were small flat jars of creams for rashes or dry skin. One side of the store was dedicated to herbal teas and medicines to ingest, while the other was strictly for external use.

The store clerk behind the counter was finishing up with a little old lady who wore her gray hair in a tight bun underneath a black hat. Her dress was black and made with beautiful lace and bead trim. I wondered if she was hot in such dark colors this time of year. My dress, on the other hand, was a pale blue and quite light. What I wouldn't give to slide into a pair of jeans and a tank.

"I'll be right with you," the clerk called out to me. That was when I realized I'd been staring at them as they finished their business.

"Oh, thanks. Take your time. I'm just looking." I picked up the first thing in front of me and found that I was reading the remedies for flatulence when the old woman startled me.

"I don't think that's your problem, dear."

When I looked up, I noticed that the woman was completely blind. Both her eyes were cloudy. The shock of it gave me a scare.

"You've lost your way and have fallen down the rabbit hole, I see."

My knees went weak and I felt paralyzed to do or say anything. What did she mean? Did she know? And was she really referring to *Alice in Wonderland*? That book wouldn't even come out until 1865, eleven years from now.

"Poor dear." She sounded sincere as she clucked under her breath.

"Miss, what may I help you with today?" The clerk had come to my rescue. His brown beard was thick, unlike the hair on his head, which was receding and sparse. Despite his hair loss, his face looked youthful. He was possibly in his thirties. "Thank you, Miss Crabtree, I'll see you the day after next."

That momentarily removed her focus from me to the man. She smiled at him like he'd just given her a lollipop before turning her attention back to me.

"Nothing here will help you, my lost little one, except..." She seemed to be changing her mind. "Try this on that arm of yours, it will help with the scarring." She was holding a small jar of cream that read: *Heal Thy Salve*. It was a blend of plantain, calendula, comfrey, coconut oil and lavender.

"If you'll excuse us, Miss Crabtree." The man was politely trying to move her along. "Good day." He guided her towards the door.

Clearly he thought she was mad.

Just as I found my voice, the bell of the door rang and Lord Henry held it open for the old lady as she walked out. He was holding a large heavy package in one hand and struggled with the door in the other. She whispered something unintelligible to him and he looked my way and then bade her farewell.

"I do apologize for that, miss. She really is a sweet old woman. I hope she didn't frighten you. We all just sort of take what she says with a grain of salt." The clerk rubbed his hands together now in anticipation of a new sale. "What can I get for you?"

"Uh…" It was hard to erase what had just happened. If this woman did know something, maybe she could help me. I panicked as she disappeared from view completely. Should I run after her? No, I would look as crazy as she did. But I needed to figure out a way to meet her again. In two days she was meant to return to the apothecary. That was what the man had said—"the day after next". I needed to find my way back here.

I realized that the man was waiting for my response. "I will take the cream Miss Crabtree suggested and something to moisturize my face." I had been missing my usual bedtime routine.

"Certainly, madame." And off the man went to wrap up my parcel.

Lord Henry joined me. "Miss Emma, whatever did you buy?" He was holding up the large package in question with some amusement. "The bookseller handed it to me when I inquired about you. Are you planning on starting a library?" His presence had already started to calm my nerves.

"Oh, you'll see. Do you think it will fit in one of those saddle bags you brought?" I hadn't thought about the transportation of it back to the house. Oops.

"We may be able to squeeze it in." He looked doubtful.

The store clerk was back with my tiny parcel. Lord Henry insisted on paying even though the money in the change purse was his money anyway. The wheels in my head were still spinning so I didn't bother to protest. Were those just the words of a crazy old woman or did she know something? I needed to find a way back here. I needed to find out what the woman meant. I needed to find a way back home.

Chapter 14

A Gift

With our errands out of the way, we decided to go for lunch at one of the two pubs in town. While nothing came of our visits to the train station and inns, as expected, bumping into Miss Crabtree had been a promising turn of events. Finally, something that gave me a surge of hope. Maybe I would discover that she was batshit crazy, but I had nothing to lose. Soon I would become a burden to my hosts and what then? Tracking the woman down would be my best chance. The challenge was going to be getting back here, but I had a day to come up with a plan.

We had settled into a table by the window at the Good Intent on College Street. The pungent smell of pipe and cigar smoke hung in the air. Beamed ceilings hung low and the wood floors were uneven, as the building had probably shifted around over the century since it had been built. It was only half past eleven and the place was already bustling. Walking in, I hadn't thought we'd find a place to sit, but on seeing Lord Henry the owner had cleared someone out and given us their table. Under normal circumstances I would probably object but my knees still felt weak from my bizarre encounter and all I could think about was a pint of beer.

A robust female cleared a path through the throngs of patrons towards us.

"All right then, today we've got a fish pie or bangers and mash, what will it be?" She was clearly very busy and hadn't taken the time to look up, but when she did she instantly registered who she was talking to and her color changed to a scarlet red. "Oh, Lord Pembrooke, I'm… obviously anything you'd like, sir, we can make it."

"That sounds fine to me." He looked to me for approval and I nodded.

As usual I was already starving. My friends always puzzled over how I managed to stay so thin given my appetite. Looking around the pub, I took in the average size of the few female patrons, making me feel like a freakish giant.

"We'll have one of each, please, and two pints of ale as well," Lord Henry said to the waitress.

When the food came, I started with the fish pie, but halfway through Lord Henry offered me some of his bangers and mash and we swapped plates. Here, no one seemed to take notice of us.

"What did that old woman say to you anyway?" My curiosity had been killing me since leaving the apothecary. He looked at me with confusion. "You know, Miss Crabtree from the apothecary."

"Oh, of course. The old woman. That poor thing. Someone ought not let her roam about unaccompanied." He laughed.

I didn't want to press him but I couldn't help but wonder what she knew. She might appear crazy to most, but I couldn't dismiss her as easily. How did she know about my arm? Was she really referring to *Alice in Wonderland* or was that just some sort of English expression—'falling down the rabbit hole'?

"I'm sorry we didn't have more success." Once again, Lord Henry looked at me apologetically and for an instant I wanted to tell him the truth. But what was the truth? Anything I said would sound as crazy as Miss Crabtree's ramblings and I didn't want to find myself locked up with the insane. *No, thanks.*

"Thank you for trying. Dr. Bainbridge seems to think my memory should start to come back by the end of the week," I said with hesitation. *That gives me very little time to sort things out.*

"Perhaps you're right, Miss Emma," he said, touching my arm. "Perhaps you are right." With a glance at his pocket watch, he stood. "I should have the grooms bring our horses around. Excuse me."

He returned to the table with the parcel tucked under his arm.

"So will you tell me what the mysterious package contains?" he asked with raised eyebrows as he settled back in his chair.

"You should open it." I swallowed my nerves. "The small books I picked up to read, but the big one is for you. I saw it in the book store and thought you might like it. Hopefully it's not one you already have."

Small butterflies fluttered around in my belly. I hadn't expected to feel so nervous about giving it to him. If I'd thought more about it I might have convinced myself not to get it in the first place. Oh, well, it was done and now I watched as he carefully undid the packaging.

"I certainly approve of your choice in literature. However, I would caution you to keep this one in your chambers," he said, holding up *Jane Eyre* and arching one dark brow for effect. Lord Henry's attention shifted to the large anatomy book.

My heart sank when he stared at it without any expression. He opened the book and scrutinized each page. I couldn't tell if he was unimpressed or simply indifferent. After an agonizing minute or two he looked at me.

"This is a most exquisite book, Miss Emma, but I cannot accept it." He had closed the book and was attempting to hand it back.

"Oh? I just thought..." I stammered. His refusal surprised me. And if I had to be honest with myself, it hurt.

"That's just it. I don't think you did. You seem to think that we have the ability to simply change our destiny because we will it so, but I can no more change mine than you can yours."

"I'm not trying to change your destiny." His reaction had taken me off guard. "I was just trying to do something nice. I saw the book and thought you might like it. That's it. Obviously I was wrong." My cheeks burned and I knew that I was turning crimson.

"It doesn't matter what I like or want, as I've told you before. I have allowed these foolish fantasies to go on long enough. My responsibilities are larger than you can imagine and I shouldn't be wasting my time indulging these frivolous pastimes."

"It seems to me that your life is in control of you instead of the other way around." As the words tumbled out of my mouth, I realized that I might have overstepped once again.

"I think you have a very strange way of looking at the world, Miss Emma." There was a coolness in his expression.

"I didn't mean..." My attempt at recovery was sloppy.

"While at times it may be charming, it is also very naive. Are you not bound by anything? Are you free to follow the wind wherever it might blow you? I think not." He finished his beer in one gulp and rose to leave.

As much as I didn't want to concede, he had a point. I was not free to choose. For now, I was stuck here, but somewhere else I had obligations, like a fiancé, and needed to get back.

"Well, I suppose you've got me there." *But it was just a book.* His refusal of my gift stung. The alcohol helped to numb some of that. These nineteenth-century men were impossible. From polite and proper to proud and stubborn in no time flat.

Moments later, I was waiting outside for Lord Henry and the groom to come out with our horses. If I'd been in my own time, I would simply have left the pub and found my own way home. I wanted to be alone to sulk.

Once we were both mounted he looked up to the sky. "We'd better move quickly if we don't want to get stuck in the rain."

Not at all what I wanted to hear. Sure enough, the patches of sunshine had now turned to doom and gloom.

"Bloody hell!" I said with irritation. Lord Henry had obviously grown accustomed to my potty mouth as he barely even flinched this time.

"My sentiments exactly," he said without humor. "We have about a thirty-minute ride if we hurry and go through the fields rather than take the main roads."

We rode on at a quick trot. Every now and then I'd look up to make sure the heavens weren't about to open. There was nothing worse than riding in the rain. Obviously growing up in L.A. I'd seldom had to consider the weather. On the rare occasion when it did rain, it poured. The entire city shut down, traffic at a standstill and every canyon with a flash flood warning. English rain was different. Most of the time it was just a constant drizzle.

Lord Henry broke into a slow canter and Angus followed suit. I gave him a little more rein and let him do as he pleased. Ten minutes in, just as I was beginning to think we'd make it, I felt the first big drop on my forehead, followed by another and another. Within seconds it was hammering down on us so hard that Angus closed his eyes to avoid the water.

"Open your eyes, you daft horse!" I scolded. Obviously he was not a fan of water.

His canter was getting stronger and stronger. Pretty soon we were in a full gallop for home with his eyes shut tight.

Oh, great.

"Emma, pull Angus up a bit!" Lord Henry shouted over the rain. The reins in my hands were slick with water and I wished in that moment I'd thought to wear my gloves.

The beer had dulled my instincts and now I simply clung to the horse's mane and hoped he knew what he was doing. The ground had turned to mud, making the footing slippery. Angus took an awkward step and started to go down.

"Emma, sit back!" bellowed Lord Henry with a mix of irritation and concern.

I sat back in the saddle and pulled hard on the reins. My horse's hindquarters came skidding under his body while his front legs struggled to find their footing. He lurched forward in an attempt to right himself. I lost my balance and slid right up his neck when he came to a sudden stop.

"Easy, boy, easy." Lord Henry had dismounted and was holding Angus' reins. With all my strength I managed to shimmy back into the saddle.

"Are you all right?" Lord Henry asked, but he looked less than amused.

"Yep. Thanks." Nothing like a slightly bruised ego to sober you up.

"Can you ride on?" He was shielding his face from the rain to avoid getting hit in the eyes as he looked up. His top hat had been lost somewhere along the way.

"I think so. Is it much farther?"

"I'm afraid it is. The White Hart is a mile away. We could wait out the rain there. Please try to keep Angus steady." His coat looked nearly soaked through and he squinted from the constant beads of water running into his eyes. If I wasn't still upset with him, I'd be able to fully appreciate how incredibly hot he looked all wet and disheveled.

"Right. Let's go." I was eager to get indoors.

Once he was mounted, I used a gentle leg to coax Angus into a walk. I knew right away something was wrong. His walk felt uneven and it wasn't because of the ground. Lord Henry noticed it too.

Chapter 15

Electricity

"It looks like he's lost a shoe." Lord Henry jumped off his mount once again and took hold of Angus. "You can ride my horse." It came out more like an order rather than an offer.

His horse was bulkier than Angus, which made straddling him difficult with my sore, tired legs. Leading both horses, Lord Henry walked briskly through the grassy field. Angus hobbled on account of his missing shoe.

The gloom outside mimicked the growing melancholy that I found myself in. As a result of being soaked to the skin, my thighs had started to chafe against the saddle, leaving them raw and tender. By the time we arrived at the White Hart, the rain had almost stopped completely. A stable boy rushed out to take our horses. Lord Henry relayed a few quick instructions before we were inside drying off by a large fire.

"Okay, now we are taking the pub crawl to a whole new level." I didn't want to act childish about Lord Henry's refusal of my gift, nor his indifference to me since then. If only April were here. She always knew how to talk me off the ledge. My eyes started to sting at the thought that I might never see her again.

"Are you in the habit of crawling to pubs then?" Lord Henry looked confused and perhaps slightly mortified.

"It's more of an expression." Not something I wished to elaborate on.

He shook off his coat and laid it out by the fire, getting ready to go order at the bar.

"Would you care for refreshments?" As if on cue, Mrs. Greasly homed in on his presence, bustling through the throngs of patrons who had either been caught out in the bad weather or had come because of it. "Oh, Lord Henry, so nice to see you back so soon," she purred. She gave me the quick up-and-down. "The earl was here for lunch, you know. It seems your mother is due."

"Stepmother," Henry corrected curtly.

"Oh, yes, of course, my apologies. Your stepmother the countess is due in today. Oh, what exciting news he did have. I suppose congratulations are in order." She gave him the equivalent of the wink-slash-elbow jab.

I looked to Lord Henry but his face gave away nothing. His expression turned to stone.

"My Sarah has left to go back to London, you know. She would have liked to give you her best wishes as well," she continued without even taking a breath.

"Ah… very well, Mrs. Greasly. May we order a drink?" He was annoyed with the woman now.

"Oh, yes, of course, of course. What can I get you, miss?" Reluctantly, she diverted her attention to me.

"Just tea, please." Definitely no more drinking.

"Brandy," Lord Henry answered before Mrs. Greasly could turn her adoration on him again. "Thank you." He sat down and looked towards the fire.

A cloud had gathered around him and it wasn't from the weather outside. Something poor Mrs. Greasly had said triggered this mood and it was growing darker by the moment.

Relieved to have the fire as a focal point, I let my own thoughts drift. The day had not been a complete waste. Meeting Miss Crabtree had given me a small ray of hope.

Mrs. Greasly returned with our drinks, humming with compliments and kind wishes. Lord Henry could no longer even bear to be civil. He stared at the fire, deep in his own misery.

For a long while we sat in silence until the young stable boy swooped in to inform us that the blacksmith had managed to fix Angus' shoe. The boy was rewarded with a shilling and after giving his profuse gratitude he walked out of the pub a little bigger in his breeches.

Suddenly eager to be on his way, Lord Henry finished his brandy in one gulp. I tried to follow suit but my tea was still too hot to do anything but take small sips so I simply abandoned it and got up to leave.

Outside the sun was shining as if it had done so all day. Only the large puddles on the ground told a different story. Angus whinnied when he saw me like I was his long-lost person. It cheered me up and pulled me out of my own melancholy state. We set off for home without a word.

"Are you all right?" I asked when I could no longer bear the silence.

"Quite fine." He was staring at the path ahead. We were sticking to the road this time.

"You don't look fine." I shouldn't have said it but it was out of my mouth before I could stop it. I wasn't sure what Mrs. Greasly meant when she said congratulations were in order but I had a distinct feeling that was the reason for this shift.

"Must you always pry, Miss Emma? I'm not entirely sure what

people are like where you're from, but here it is considered impertinent to concern yourself in others' affairs."

"The stiff-upper-lip thing you Brits are known for is nonsense. Where I'm from, it's actually considered healthy to share your thoughts with others, not this ridiculous practice of keeping everything bottled up inside." My irritation took a hold of me. "So if you want to talk about it I'm all ears, otherwise, don't take it out on me. You're hardly the only one with problems."

Lord Henry was about to respond but instead I kicked Angus and rode straight past him. I didn't want to follow in his wake a moment longer. His bad mood was rubbing off on me. That was what I told myself anyway, but I knew there was some other reason I needed to get away from him. I was starting to care. And when he was upset it tore me up. But why? I hardly knew the man and yet I felt I knew him all too well.

He continued always a horse length behind, no doubt stewing over his own troubles and perhaps cursing himself for having the misfortune of my company. Both of which I could do nothing about.

For the remainder of the ride I fell into a hypnotic state, listening to the sound of the horse hooves on the hard-packed dirt road. The smell of wet grass from the adjacent fields was like sweet perfume. My body ached from exhaustion, both emotional and physical. We plodded along until I recognized the canopy of trees and I knew the Dormer House was just around the bend.

The closer we got the more anxious I started to feel. Angus picked up on it immediately. His own step changed in anticipation of some perceived danger. His ears perked forward and a loud snort of the air revealed nothing, but he was on alert. Horses were so good at reading people's emotions. Animals of flight. I could identify with that instinct. Had I not built a life avoiding the things that were difficult or dangerous?

The stable was quiet when we arrived, all the horses nibbling away at their dinner. The young groom, Jamie, bounded in to relieve us of our mounts. Reluctantly, I handed over the reins. I had hoped to untack Angus myself and let his soothing energy wash over me and calm my nerves.

Without a word, Lord Henry stormed off to the house. With his chores done, Jamie scurried off to his supper. Instead of heading back to the house, I wandered over to the mare and her foal and stood by their stall door watching them. This day had been full of discoveries and I needed time to process it all. What had Miss Crabtree meant? Did she know? What was eating away at Lord Henry? Was I really so naive about the world? Maybe the gift had been foolish. I felt silly for having gone out on a limb like that. I had only thought to please him and instead I'd contributed to his misery. Why did I want to please him so much? Was it gratitude for everything he'd done? Or something else? Something I didn't want to acknowledge.

The foal was standing under the mare suckling while she nuzzled his hind end, creating wet circles with her lips. I wished I could collapse into the comfort of a mother. *My mother.* It had been years since I'd allowed myself to think of her that way for fear that I wouldn't be able to stop the longing. Maybe it was the exhaustion, but I stood watching for a long time, soaking up the bond between the two as if I were connected to it. And when the tears started to fall, I simply let them stream down my face until my vision blurred and it started to tickle and itch. Without a tissue, I used my sleeve to dab at them.

"Here, use this." Lord Henry startled me. He was standing next to me with a linen handkerchief in hand.

"Oh, God! How long have you been standing there?" I tried to hide my face. He pressed the handkerchief to my open palm. It smelt of lavender.

"Not long." His expression had softened from earlier. "I hope I didn't upset you?"

I kept my eyes from looking his way, still embarrassed to be caught crying. I felt a stab of annoyance at myself for letting my guard down. Ben always thought I looked weak or dramatic if I cried in front of him. Shame burned the tips of my ears and I shook it off almost as quickly as I had the thoughts of my mother. It was always about survival.

"No, nothing like that." I waved him off and used the handkerchief to dab my eyes dry. "Are you always so stealthy?"

"My intention was not to startle you. Then I noticed you were…" He looked unsure how to finish his thought. "Are you angry with me?"

"Not at all. Just trying to process the day."

His brows were slightly furrowed with concern.

"Really, I'm fine."

Instinctively I touched his arm as a sign of reassurance and realized he was standing so close. His muscles tensed under my hand and I wondered if I'd given him a shock. My friends used to tease me that I had a constant surge at my fingertips.

When I looked up, he was watching me, his expression quite serious. This suddenly increased my awareness of the diminished space between us, that distance reserved for intimacy. Every extremity of my body tingled. As I looked from his eyes to his perfect lips, the energy around us was charged and dangerous. My hand, which was still touching his arm, failed to let go. I could not have willed it to do so. Instead, that small physical connection served as a conductor for the electricity building within us.

He raised his other hand to brush stray strands of hair from my face and I felt a flutter deep inside me. That was when the shift happened. I knew I should turn away, like I did with most things I didn't want to acknowledge. But I couldn't move away from him. Only towards him.

I wasn't sure who made the first move—it could have been me—but before I knew it my lips were on his. They felt warm and familiar, like coming home. My arms wrapped around his neck, pulling him closer, and his in turn squeezed the air out of me. My head swam with excitement and need and something else I'd never felt. Our kiss pulsed with urgency.

It might have lasted only seconds, but Lord Henry pulled away first. Both of us were breathless. I'd never in my life experienced anything in the same stratosphere. My first kiss with Ben had felt mechanical by comparison. It had taken many awkward attempts before it was even pleasant. Passionate would never have been a word to describe it. This, on the other hand, was turbulent, like two ships colliding in a rough sea, and now I was standing in the middle of the wreckage.

"I cannot, Miss Emma." His warm breath grazed my cheek but his eyes wavered and struggled to meet mine. A look of shame filled his expression as he untangled himself from my embrace. My lips felt swollen and I touched them to make sure they were intact because they continued to buzz with excitement. For a moment, I stood there speechless. I felt exposed.

"Of course. I'm sorry. I don't know what…" Flustered and embarrassed, I didn't know how to finish my sentence or where to look. While I hadn't kissed many guys, no one had ever swept me off my feet like this, leaving me panting and wanting.

"I apologize for my ungentlemanly behavior." He took a step away from me, out of the danger zone, and straightened his jacket. "There are things you must know."

"Please don't," I whispered and put a hand up to stop his explanation, as it would undoubtedly make me feel even worse than

I already did. Rejection was something I always took personally. "Why were you here anyway?" I asked with a forced edge in my voice.

He cleared his throat, still visibly shaken and uncomfortable.

"When Phoebus told me you hadn't yet returned I came looking for you. My stepmother has arranged a dinner for this evening and wishes you to join us. There will be some company attending, so Miss Barnsby will find you something suitable to wear." Now he was back to business as usual. He had taken another small step away from me.

"I guess I should get cleaned up then." I picked up the packages that I had bought in Oxwich that day, including the medical book that had been declined, and made my way towards the house at a brisk walk. Lord Henry called something out to me but I didn't hear it, nor did I turn back and wait for him.

Chapter 16

Talking Walls

I felt like a fool. Never had I wanted to crawl out of my own skin as much as I did now. What had come over me in the stables? Lord Henry had awoken something inside me that had long been dormant. Now I struggled to act as if nothing had happened. How could I have humiliated myself like that? What had I been thinking? Was it loneliness? Sitting at a large dinner table with a room full of strangers was not the best place to regroup.

There were several people dining with us this evening. The Weatherfields, who came with their two teenage daughters, were the first to arrive, followed closely by some old baron and baroness well into their seventies, whose name I never got as everyone simply called them by their title. Then came Lord and Lady Windthrob, both of whom were as wide as they were tall, and each held a handkerchief over their noses.

"It's the cholera," Lady Windthrob explained when she came in. "It's dreadfully scary in London at the moment."

Now both she and her husband were settled at the table talking through their embroidered linen hankies to Sir Thomas Sigmore and his very young female companion. I'd assumed she was his daughter until I overheard talk of their impeding nuptials.

"Are you to be married in London?" Lady Windthrob asked Sir Thomas, crumbs falling from her lips from her dinner roll.

"Yes, before Christmas, and then it's off to the Continent for our honeymoon," he said proudly, giving his fiancée a nod.

"Let's just hope this cholera doesn't ruin your plans," she said, looking quite concerned. "My husband and I aren't taking any chances. We're very careful to cover our faces and not breathe any unpleasant odors. Who knows how far-reaching this outbreak could be."

Listening to their conversation, I couldn't help but put in my two cents.

"You can't catch cholera from the air," I said, trying to be helpful and hopefully set this poor woman at ease. "It's from contaminated…"

All eyes at the table had turned to me. Conversations had ceased mid-sentence. I realized my mistake all too late.

"… water," I finished, feeling much less confident.

Everyone looked at the pitcher of water standing untouched in the center of the table. The earl broke the silence by launching into a belly laugh. Others joined in, less certain but wanting to be in on the joke. My cheeks burned with humiliation. Lord Henry's eyes brushed over me with sympathy.

"Miss Emma, I've never heard such a ridiculous thing," the earl said, wiping tears from his face. I knew he didn't mean it maliciously but he was clearly still a strong believer in the miasma theory that diseases like that were caused by pollution or bad air. John Snow was about to discover the real cause of cholera and announce it to the world. Lucky for me, everyone in the room thought I was crazy. In the future, I'd have to be more careful.

Once the dust had settled, Lord Henry's friend Lieutenant John Walker breezed in with profound apologies for his tardiness and was seated in the empty chair next to me. With nearly twenty people at the table, I struggled to keep track of them all.

Edmund, Lord Henry's brother, was having a one-way conversation with the baron. Edmund looked nothing like either of his siblings. He was a scrawny young man with crooked teeth and a sullen disposition. It was his bad breath that had struck me when I was first introduced to him. Now I watched as the baron politely tried to shield himself from the unpleasant odor. It was a relief not to be seated next to him.

Course upon course was brought to the table with more cutlery than I ever knew existed. I took my lead from Isobel, Lord Henry's sister, to see what utensil to use next. She was conveniently seated across from me at the table. I paid close attention to her impeccable manners.

She couldn't be more than eighteen years old, but she was already a lady of the house. Her hair was dark brown, much like Lord Henry's, but her nose was small and her face full of freckles. Not what you'd consider beautiful, but pleasant. Much kinder-looking than her mother, whose manner seemed somewhat austere. With her black hair tied back in a tight bun, her mother's face looked stern and skeletal. Her dark eyes were catlike, not in their shape as much as in the way they watched you, with judgment and distance.

Mr. and Mrs. Weatherfield were very well dressed. She was so bejeweled that I wondered if she often suffered back or neck pain as a result of the exorbitant display of wealth she adorned herself with. One of their daughters, Jane, was seated next to Lord Henry. She had pretty blonde hair but a very large Roman nose and a serious lack of a chin. She spoke only when spoken to. Mostly, she listened intently to every word that Lord Henry said, even when it was not directed at her, which was most of the time.

The explanation given for my presence was that I was a distant relation on holiday. The countess was worried that any semblance of the truth might leave a scandalous taste in their guests' mouths, so she felt it was best to lie. I wasn't sure if the guests actually believed it or if they thought I was from a less notable branch of the family.

Following my disruption, no one directed the slightest curiosity or interest my way. That was, no one except for Lieutenant John Walker, who looked as much an outcast as I felt. He was a very handsome man somewhere in his twenties, with sandy hair that fell in curvy waves just below his ears. His face was chiseled like a Greek statue's and his body built like a football player's, stocky and muscular. He was easy on the eyes, but aware of it. He spoke under his breath often and I never knew if he was talking to me or had a nervous habit that I should try to ignore.

At one end of the table, the countess recounted some of the current London gossip and scandals, while at the other the earl was debating the wisdom of having more laws concerning children in the workforce. He felt that even more stringent restriction could negatively affect business. Was he really so heartless?

"If Lady Windthrob has one more roll I'm afraid she won't fit out that door," Lieutenant Walker said close to my ear.

My hand flew to my mouth to stifle a laugh. He was right though. The woman was enormous. Like Middle American carnival-going kind of enormous with bad teeth to boot.

"Do you always make fun of people like this?" I whispered back through my napkin.

"Does it bother you?" One perfect brow arched. Challenging. Playful.

On the outside, Miss Barnsby had worked her magic and I looked acceptable. However, inside I felt like a hot mess. So many things had happened today and my emotions were flying around inside me like confetti, my kiss with Lord Henry taking on the greater share.

Where did Ben fit into to all of this? What did that make me? *A cheater*. Was I a terrible person? If I were being honest with myself, what troubled me most was not my infidelity but Lord Henry's rejection. In this moment I wanted to avoid men, even the handsome one sitting next to me trying to be charming, but I could feel my resolve weakening.

"Not at all. Given the circumstances, it's entertaining," I admitted to the lieutenant.

"Well, I'm glad I could oblige, Miss Emma." He had obviously taken my comment as encouragement. "Are you enjoying your time at Dormer House? Has my dear friend Henry been hospitable and shown you the sights?"

"Is there more to it than rolling hills and country pubs?" I was feeling the full effects of the wine now. Maybe being a little bit flirty with a stranger was better than wallowing in my own self-pity.

"So you've seen the best country life has to offer then," he said without a hint of sarcasm and we both laughed.

"How do you know Lord Henry?" I asked, hoping to make polite conversation.

"We were at Eton together," he said, and I raised an inquisitive brow at him. "They called us tugs in those days."

"What was that?" I asked.

"As King's Scholars we were forced to wear a black overcoat with tails. It was silly really." He bit off a piece of dinner roll as he spoke. "The other boys loved to give them a tug when the headmaster wasn't looking. Hence the name 'tugs'." He poured us both another glass of wine without asking.

"That's embarrassing." I couldn't imagine Lord Henry getting teased.

"On the contrary, we were quite pleased with ourselves at thirteen, being two of only seventy kids across the country with such a distinction. Henry even wore his tails to bed sometimes." We both laughed at the thought.

My eyes drifted to Lord Henry and I caught him looking at us. Instead of smiling he looked away. I refused to allow myself any more torture over what had passed between us.

It wasn't until the meal was coming to an end and the tables were being cleared to make room for dessert that the reason for the formal dinner was revealed. A light tapping on a wine glass brought everyone's attention to the head of the table where the earl was seated.

"I would like to thank everyone for coming tonight. The countess and I would like to congratulate the newly engaged couple."

While I looked to Sir Thomas with a congratulatory smile, the earl raised his glass to Lord Henry and the Weatherfields' eldest daughter Jane, who blushed and raised her hand to her chest as if overcome with emotion.

A piece of tough meat I'd been trying to break down for the better half of twenty minutes found its way to the back of my throat and I started to choke. Lieutenant Walker, with his quick military reflexes, smacked me on my back and the offending piece of steak flew out of my mouth into my napkin. Only the countess noticed the fuss, which she rewarded with a scolding look.

"As we are very anxious to welcome Jane to the family," the earl continued without even a glance my way, "and in honor of this union, we will be holding an engagement ball here at Dormer House in two days' time. Our annual hunt this season, on the twenty-second of August, I believe it is"—he looked to the countess, who simply nodded her acceptance—"will also serve to celebrate the coming together of these two great families, the Drakes and Weatherfields. "He lifted his glass to indicate that he was done with the speech and downed it without delay.

Though I had recovered from my poorly timed choke, I couldn't help but feel gutted by the announcement. So much so that I couldn't even look at Lord Henry, although I felt his eyes on me more than once. It was *just* a kiss, I reminded myself. Maybe that was what he had tried to tell me in the stable.

Of course.

I'd been so foolish. In all the craziness of the last few days, not only had I allowed myself to get swept up in this world in which I didn't belong, but more importantly, I'd forgotten Lord Henry's tragic fate. He would never marry Jane because he'd be dead long before the wedding. Alarm shot through my body and sobered me instantly.

Isobel noticed the change in my expression. I forced a smile for her benefit. Sometime soon her brother would die. *What was the date?* Instinctively, my hand went for the pocket where I normally kept my iPhone but of course it wasn't there. Old habits died hard. It was only days away, if I remembered correctly. I stole a quick glance at Lord Henry, who looked like he was suffering a bout of indigestion. Soon he would suffer far more than that.

When dinner was officially over, Lord Henry's sister singled me out and encouraged me to join the ladies in the great parlor. The men were going to remain at the table smoking cigars.

"This is the part where they congratulate each other on being men," Isobel whispered in my ear. It was in that instant that I realized how much I liked this girl. "You know, that dress suits you much better than it ever did me. I think it's because you are so fair. If you like it, you should keep it," she said.

The dress was a beautiful shade of light green. The lace around the low neckline was also beaded. "Thank you. You have great taste." I returned the compliment. Finally in a sea of unfriendly faces it felt nice to be shown kindness. She had already managed to lift my spirits.

Isobel and I stuck to our own corner talking. She told me about London and how much she loved it there.

"Have you been there?" She clapped a hand to her mouth. "I'm so sorry, Miss Emma, of course you wouldn't remember if you had. I didn't mean to appear insensitive to your… your condition."

"No harm done," I replied. The London I had been to had been nothing like her London anyway, so I guessed I really hadn't been.

Sensing that I was becoming a bit too familiar with her daughter, the countess made her way over.

"Isobel, leave us a moment, dear." She said this without taking her eyes off me, like a cat hunting its prey.

Isobel shot me a concerned look when she got up.

"So tell me, Miss Clayton, where exactly are you from?" The countess settled on the edge of a chair, indicating that our little rendezvous would be brief. Plastered on her face was a tight smile, the kind people offered when their patience had already run out.

"Um… America?" Was this a trick question?

The countess was a very well-preserved woman in her forties who hardly ever seemed to blink. Her face also didn't vary much in the way of expression, like many of the plastic surgery addicts in Beverly Hills.

"Of course, dear, but from where? I know a great deal of families in America." She emphasized the last syllable of America.

"Ahhh, Los Angeles." I watched her search her memory for such a place.

"I'm not as familiar with the small villages. When did you arrive in England? Do you remember that?"

Now I was starting to sweat because I felt like she was trying to catch me in a lie rather than ask out of interest. "I don't remember much, really…"

"So I've been told." She cut me off. "Do you know what brought you here?"

I decided to go for half truths. "My mother was from here. In the north. Although we lost touch with her family some time ago." As soon as it was out of my mouth, I knew I'd revealed too much.

"And what would her name be?" Her black eyes narrowed in anticipation.

"Eileen Farrar." I doubted the countess planned to track down my mother's family.

"I don't know that family." She seemed to be searching her memory. "Well, I doubt they travel in the same social circles." She scanned the room almost to emphasize our current company before returning her full attention back to me. Her comment stung, as I was sure it was intended to. "Amazing that you are able to recall names, but not where you were living here."

"Yes, the doctor felt it was sometimes common with head injuries." Beads of sweat started to pool on my brow and I resisted the urge to wipe them with my hand. The last thing I wanted was even more scrutiny. Desperate to get this woman off my tail, I decided to shift the conversation. "You have a beautiful home. I am so thankful for the wonderful hospitality." My cheeks hurt from the forced smiles.

"Oh, yes. My son Edmund is very charming, is he not? He is also betrothed to someone equally suitable." She said this as if I might have designs on Edmund, who had the personality of a turnip as far as I'd seen and was about as attractive as one.

"How nice for him. She's a lucky girl." Kill her with kindness was my internal mantra, my stage smile perfected.

"Yes, luckier than that poor little Jane, to be sure." She looked over at the girl now with a look of pity. "She'll have her work cut out trying to fit that one into the mold of an earl. Takes after his mother,

I hear. Not quite as refined as one ought to be."

My hackles were immediately up. "I wouldn't say that at all. Lord Henry will make a terrific earl and he takes his responsibilities very seriously, not to mention he is compassionate and..."

"Ah. I see you seem to have quite an understanding of my stepson in such a short time. You may want to consider bestowing your affections where they are appropriate though, don't you think? After all, he is soon to be married." Condescension dripped from her every word.

"I didn't mean—" I felt flustered. "I wasn't trying to say..."

"Be assured I know everything that goes on, Miss Clayton. After all, I am the lady of the house and even my walls talk if I ask them to." She motioned around the room as she smiled a very toothy smile at me and I felt the full effect of looking into a lion's mouth. She rose to leave, but seemed to have one last thing to share. "I'm so glad we had a chance to get to know one another. I do hope we are able to reunite you with your family soon." In a swoosh of fine clothes she left and I couldn't help feeling like I'd made my first enemy.

Chapter 17

Kiss and Tell

That night I dreamt of lions and tigers and bears. I was Dorothy trying to find my way out of Oz and back to Kansas, only along the way I found myself frolicking with Lord Henry, the soon-to-be-married Englishman, in a tall patch of clovers.

When I woke up it was still dark. At first I felt annoyed to be pulled out of such an erotic dream. Guilt quickly followed for having enjoyed it at all. After what happened with Lord Henry, I hadn't even had time to think of Ben. What did that mean? I had cheated on my fiancé and I should feel torn up about it. Never in my life had I been that girl, but yet here I was throwing myself at the first man I met.

Today I had to figure out how I was going to get back to Oxwich and track down Miss Crabtree. I couldn't very well steal a horse. If I walked I could probably make it in about three hours. Definitely an option, but I still needed to tell people why I needed to go.

The book. I could return the book I'd given Henry. Maybe leaving before anyone woke up would make life easier. Could I find my way in the dark? I wasn't sure I should risk it. Either way, I had a whole day to figure it out. She was only due at the apothecary tomorrow.

Since I was wide awake, I decided to go down to the library and browse through some of the books. Without Miss Barnsby's help, I struggled into my clothes, never entirely sure if I was doing it right.

I tiptoed down the stairs, cautious after the last time I had come down in search of food and found myself labeled a thief. The double doors to the library stood slightly ajar. The musty smell of aging paper and worn leather book covers welcomed me in. A flurry of sudden movement caught my eye. Isobel, in a passionate embrace with a young man, gasped when she saw me. Wisps of red hair escaped his ponytail. They were fully clothed but judging by their expressions they might as well have been naked.

It had all happened so fast and I felt terrible walking in on them. Both looked like scared teenagers caught having sex by a father with a shotgun.

"I'm so sorry," I said, breaking the awkward silence that ensued. "I'll just..."

"No, it's I who must apologize," the young man said to me, as he straightened his clothes and readjusted himself. A deep scar ran the length of his jaw, giving him a roguish look. "I must be going." He looked nervously at Isobel and bowed to her. "Lady Isobel."

"Mr. White." She nodded to him as if he was being released from her service.

In a deer-like flurry of limbs, he dashed past me and slipped out the open window before I could say anything else.

"Isobel, I had no idea..." I started to say, when the earl came in and found both Isobel and I looking slightly stunned.

"Who is here? Was there a gentleman in this room?" He looked at Isobel for answers and ignored me completely. "I heard a man's voice." He was still dressed in his clothes from the previous evening, only they looked crinkled and bulging, like he'd fallen asleep somewhere and not made it to bed. Where had the earl been at this hour?

Isobel sat perched on the lounge chair, paralyzed. I wasn't sure what kind of nineteenth-century wrath would be unleashed on a young woman caught fooling around, but I assumed it would be far worse than anything in my lifetime.

"Sorry, sir, I mean, Lord." I felt like a babbling idiot under pressure. "That was me. I came in to look for a book and woke Lady Isobel. I must have startled her."

"I heard a man's voice." He looked at me, challenging me to disagree.

"Well, I do sound quite manly at this hour in the morning. My throat is a bit hoarse." I coughed to show him.

He scrutinized me and then turned his gaze back to his daughter.

"It is true, Father." Isobel took up the lie I'd started as if it were her own. "I must have fallen asleep here and Miss Clayton gave me quite a start." She looked at him, the image of innocence, her hand now resting on her chest like she was still trying to calm her frayed nerves.

"All right then. My apologies." He left us and went upstairs, presumably to his room. When he was out of earshot Isobel and I both let out the breaths we had been holding.

"Miss Emma, you have saved me. I am forever in your debt." Her face had started to regain color.

"I'm so sorry I walked in on you like that. I had no idea anyone was even up yet." If this had been my friend April I would have peppered her with questions straight away.

Isobel gave a little guilty giggle. "I hate to imagine what would have happened if my father had discovered us." We both played that out in our minds and frowned at the idea. "Well, I'm sure he's had his fair share of indiscretions. Clearly he has not just come from his own bedchamber."

So Mr. Uptight Earl was a wanderer. I imagined him with Miss

Barnsby bent over the dining table and then shook my head to erase the image.

"So who was that boy? I think I'm entitled to a little gossip." I watched as she considered my request.

She motioned me to sit next to her with a delicate hand while she adjusted herself more comfortably on the lounge chair, preparing to spill the beans. We sat no more than a couple feet apart.

"His name is William. He is so lovely. I think he's been in love with me for some time, but wouldn't admit it until recently. You know how men can be?" She took a deep breath as if to savor a memory of him. "We grew up together, you see. We used to play in the stables and on the grounds. We were inseparable. That scar on his cheek was from playing sticks," she said with a proud grin. "Eventually my governess told my parents that it was unnatural for a girl to play with a boy, and with someone of his inferior birth no less. They were worried my delicate sensibilities would become corrupted, that's what I overheard them saying. So he was sent off to school. And that was the last I saw of him."

"That's sad." I couldn't help but think of all the friends I'd had growing up who were from different socioeconomic backgrounds. Most of the time I'd even preferred the company of the boys to the girls in our neighborhood. I was such a tomboy.

"Yes, it was. We wrote for a while but eventually that stopped. We lost touch for years until we bumped into each other at the market in Oxwich last spring. He's working in a law firm in town."

"So what's going on with you now?" It sounded like such a sweet love story.

"That's it, I'm afraid. My parents would never entertain the idea of a courtship between us." She looked at me like I had just lost my mind.

"Why not, if you love him?"

"Don't be silly, Emma." She gave my knee an affectionate squeeze. "He doesn't have any land or titles. What kind of future could I ever expect to have?"

"Oh… I see." Of course I should have clued in.

"He's studying to be a barrister and the best he could do is make partner for Heany, Blake and Sons." She pulled a pendant from inside her bosom and showed me. "He brought me this." A smile returned to her face. It was a woven metal charm, like a birdcage, with what looked like a bird breaking free.

"It's beautiful." I held it up to admire it in the dim light.

"Yes, it is," she said before tucking it back into her cleavage. "He is very sweet."

"That's why he was here?" I asked and Isobel blushed.

"Oh, Emma, it's just hopeless." One tear escaped her eye and slowly made its way down her face like a snail, leaving a slimy path in its wake. "Every time I think I should put a stop to his false hopes, I can't bring myself to do it. He seems to have this power over me. When we are together it feels so nice and I know in my heart that I am his. I just want to hold on to that feeling for a little longer."

Her words made me think of Lord Henry and then I wondered why they didn't make me think of Ben.

Chapter 18

A Distraction

Isobel and I made plans to go shopping in town later that day. With breakfast finished, I retreated to my room in an effort to avoid Lord Henry.

Isobel's troubles over William hit a little too close to home. I couldn't quite make sense of the feelings I had for Lord Henry. Therefore, the easiest course of action was to avoid dangerous territory completely. A budding friendship with Isobel offered a welcome distraction. It felt nice to be myself without being scrutinized or judged. Just like Henry, she wore a mask around her family and behaved as she was expected to, hardly ever showing any kind of displeasure.

There was a knock at my door, but before I could even answer, Isobel came fluttering in with her arms full of garments and gowns.

"What's all this?" I asked, not sure if I was in the mood for a fashion show.

"We have to find you something beautiful to wear for the ball tomorrow." She heaved the massive pile onto my bed and turned to size me up.

"Am I supposed to be there?" The truth was I had no desire to be part of the festivities and rather hoped that my inclusion would be overlooked.

"Well, of course you are. I checked with Mama and she insists." Isobel looked happy to have me as her charge and I didn't want to disappoint her.

"Oh, yeah, a ball, just like Cinderella." I mimicked enthusiasm.

"I love that story. You've read the Grimm Brothers then? I much prefer the original French version, *Cendrillon*." She snapped her fingers and spun around. "So I shall be your fairy godmother," she said and we both laughed.

Isobel picked up the first dress on the top of the pile. It was a peach silk with dark lace trim and a gazillion ruffles. She held it up to herself and danced around the room. "What do you think?"

Then she lifted an oyster-colored dress to her chest and when my eyes didn't light up she tossed it down too and picked up the next one.

"You should try this one on. I think it would accentuate your eyes." It was a light green chiffon. My eyes were considered hazel but when I cried or wore certain colors they turned green.

Not wanting to be Debbie Downer, I stripped off. I was halfway out of my clothes when Isobel gasped. "What is that?" She sounded intrigued.

I looked down to my navel and realized that she was referring to my tattoo. It had been a part of my body for so long now that I hardly ever remembered that it was there. "A bird," I said, feeling uncomfortable under the microscope. She came a little closer to inspect it.

"I can see it's a bird, but I've never seen such a thing painted on a woman's body." She looked at it like a child examining an exotic bug for the first time, with wonder and amazement.

"It's called a tattoo and it's not really painted on. They use small needles filled with ink so that it doesn't wash off." It was a silly thing I'd done on a whim with some friends. We'd made a teenage pact to all get one, only once I was finished everyone else had chickened out. With only one visible wing it was a bit of an unusual-looking bird. I'd doodled it during one of my classes and was quite proud of it at the time. As soon as it was done I'd wished I hadn't done it, but there was no turning back. The painful process of having it removed didn't seem worth it, not to mention the expense of it. Hardly anyone even knew I had it. Even my father had never found out.

Isobel came even closer. She reached her hand out to me. "May I touch it?" Never taking her eyes off the tattoo, she reached a delicate hand towards me.

"Sure."

Her hands were cool.

"I want one too!" she declared with a smile. "Did it hurt?" She continued to stare at it like it would somehow move on its own.

"A little, but not too much." I could imagine Isobel at a tattoo parlor in L.A. She would be blown away by all the possibilities.

"Maybe they do such things in London. I will have to look into it." She got up and we resumed our task at hand. I wiggled into the dress while Isobel helped button me up. Without all the necessary undergarments it didn't look great, but you could get an idea.

We continued like this, laughing and chatting like old friends. More than once she reminded me of April with her wit and humor. The final dress was the winner in the end. Of course, I felt like it was completely over the top, but Isobel was so excited that I didn't have the heart to refuse.

That being done, we decided to leave for tea. Isobel rang for Miss Barnsby and rattled off some instructions for the dress.

It was nice to get out of the house. A veil of drizzle left the air cool and brimming with the earthy smell of freshly raked leaves. Isobel had McCleary bring up the Brougham, which was a beautiful red carriage that sat only two people, with a covered roof. It was a much nicer option than the one we'd taken to Oxwich, as the seats were forward-facing with a clear view of the road ahead.

The household had been a busy hive of activity with the preparations for the ball. No one seemed too worried about our departure, least of all the countess, who was clearly in her element barking out instructions to the staff and reprimanding those who were found by her elevated standards to be incompetent. Hopefully it would be this easy for me to set out tomorrow.

"What happened to your hand?" I asked Isobel when I noticed that her right hand was bandaged.

"I cut myself on some glass. It was extremely clumsy of me. There was blood everywhere; a complete disaster. And I nearly ruined one of my favorite dresses."

"Poor you." Her dramatics suggested it was far more serious than I imagine it was.

"No matter. I can still manage," she said in case I was worried we'd have to call off our excursion.

The village of Foxford sat on the edge of two merging rivers. A flint stone bridge crossed the length of both and was wide enough for two carriages to pass side by side. McCleary dropped us off at the far side of the small square, where a cute collection of shops lined the streets. Isobel dragged me straight for Delilah's, which was a ladies' store specializing in accessories, everything from hats to ribbons to gloves.

We hadn't noticed Jane, Henry's fiancée, when we walked in but we certainly did now as she made a show about leaving. Many eager young girls scrambled around her, hoping that her good fortune might rub off on them or that perhaps she would be kind enough to bestow even an ounce of friendship on them. She looked overwhelmed by the attention and waited for them to clear out of her way before leaving with her mother and a small entourage. Half the place emptied out in her wake, as most of the women were curious about Lord Henry's wife-to-be.

Isobel rolled her eyes at me, a look that was not lost on Jane as she walked out the door. It was clear that Isobel disliked Jane. She wasn't gaining a sister in this union but an inconvenience, according to her. Everything about Jane had been learned in a book—how to behave, what to say, whom to talk to. She was a doll. That was how Isobel described her. At great length.

"Honestly, Emma, she's pathetic." Isobel said as she ran her good hand over the ribbons.

I didn't feel the same way. Of course, a small part of me wanted to hate her for being engaged to a man I had feelings for, but she was a tool in all this. From what I'd heard, the first time she'd even met Lord Henry was at last night's dinner. Did she even have a choice whether or not to marry? Maybe she had her own hopes and dreams but wasn't able to share them. I had to think she was more than the picture Isobel painted of her.

The shop owner, Mrs. Tinkly, was an elegant-looking woman in her forties. With the patience of a saint, she waited on Isobel hand and foot while I strolled around, looking at and touching all the fabrics.

"That looks lovely on you, Lady Isobel," Mrs. Tinkly remarked as she held two other bonnets in her hand.

"What do you think, Emma?" Isobel asked as if Mrs. Tinkly had not spoken.

"I think she's right. It really brings out your eye color." I wasn't sure what people looked for in a bonnet. To be honest, it was a little too *Little House on the Prairie* for me.

"All right, I'll take both of them, the gloves and the ribbons too," Isabel said to the shop owner, never taking her eyes off her reflection in the small mirror.

"Terrific choices. I'll have those wrapped right away," Mrs. Tinkly said with enthusiasm. "Will you be putting these on account?"

"Yes. My friend will have to sign for me, though, as I've injured my hand." She turned towards me. "Emma, do you mind?"

"Of course not," I said, walking to join Mrs. Tinkly as she prepared the paperwork.

"You can sign here"—she pointed to a blank space on the paper—"and here." She indicated a separate paper.

I did as I was told and she handed Isobel one of the copies.

"Emma," Isobel called out to me. "I bought the second one for you to wear now. You can't go around with your hair flying around like that. Consider it a little gift."

"Thank you," I said. "You didn't have to." I wasn't sure if I should feel insulted or touched.

"That's what friends do for each other." She smiled and handed me the hat that Mrs. Tinkly was holding out to me. It was not the most flattering of colors on me, but I accepted the gift graciously.

As we walked out of the shop, we both noticed Lieutenant Walker heading our way. He hadn't yet noticed us and I considered whisking Isobel in the opposite direction, but before I could, she made a big fuss trying to wave him over. I really wished she hadn't. I wasn't sure that I was in the mood. When he asked if we'd join him for a drink at the Hare and Whistle, Isobel accepted without a moment's hesitation.

"You don't mind, Emma, do you?" she whispered to me as an afterthought.

There was a moment of awkwardness when the lieutenant pulled out a chair and Isobel made a gracious move to sit until he indicated for her to sit around the other side. A chubby drunkard named Joe was patting the seat next to him. Something passed over her face, but in seconds it was gone and replaced by her charming smile. The taste of beer was welcome and before long we were all enjoying a much-needed laugh.

"Tell me, Miss Clapton, will you be attending the ball tomorrow evening?" the lieutenant asked me in a hushed voice, as if he didn't already know.

"It's Clayton," I corrected. "And yes, I'll be there. Will you?"

"Only to be in your presence once again." He took my hand and kissed it. "Would you do me the honor of a dance tomorrow then?" His eyes lingered on something outside before turning his gaze back to me.

"Sure," I answered only to be polite, but hoped he wouldn't hold me to it.

When he released my hand I took hold of my glass. A small part of me felt flattered by the attention, especially in the wake of Lord Henry's rejection. I figured there was no harm in that. Isobel had settled into a conversation at the other end of the table and seemed to be enjoying herself.

A few drinks later, I found myself leaning heavily into the lieutenant as he escorted Isobel and I to our carriage. He was making us both laugh with his impersonations of the countess. As one of Henry's oldest friends, he'd known the family for a long time and was able to imitate her pursed-lip speech flawlessly.

"John," came a familiar deep voice. Lord Henry's expression registered surprise when he saw me on the lieutenant's arm. He scowled down at us from horseback. "I won't have time for a drink after all. I just came to tell Isobel that her mother seeks a word with her."

"Surely you didn't come all this way to deliver a message to your sister. Come now, old boy, let's have a proper catch-up." Despite the large amount of ale already consumed, the lieutenant barely even swayed.

"Another time perhaps. When my time is less restricted. I've got much to do before my engagement party." Henry hardly glanced my way but I felt the weight of his words on my heart, which felt pierced like a pincushion in my chest.

With his messages delivered he turned and trotted off. Not towards Dormer House but away from it. A sense of dread burned in my belly. My stomach felt turned upside down. Why did I feel like I'd just been caught with my hand in the cookie jar? Most importantly, why did I care so much what Lord Henry thought?

"Oh, great. What does Mother want now?" Isobel didn't remark on her brother's manner; she was more irritated that she had been summoned.

"Well, ladies, I bid you farewell and look forward to our continued acquaintance tomorrow evening." Lieutenant Walker bowed his head to us and went back to the pub.

A weak smile crossed my lips. How could I celebrate Lord Henry's union with another?

Chapter 19

Ladies Do Lunch

It was amazing to see how quickly the house was readied for the ball. The large formal sitting room, which was really like two very large rooms in one, was stripped of furniture, making a large area for dancing and mingling.

Even though I wasn't keen to celebrate Lord Henry's engagement, the energy in the household was infectious. What an experience to be part of such an event in a house like this. Of course I'd seen *Pride and Prejudice* at least a dozen times but now I was going to see what these things were really like, not just the Hollywood version. The dining room was set up as a large buffet area where platters of food would be laid out for the guests to nibble on. Extra footmen from nearby estates had been called in for the evening to help serve and clear.

All morning wagons had been making deliveries with fresh meat, cheese, general supplies and casks of wine and whiskey. It was exciting to be a fly on the wall observing the scale of the preparations. I couldn't even imagine what would be done for the wedding.

Lord Henry's tragic accident registered in my mind and stopped me in my tracks. They wouldn't need to worry about any wedding preparations in the end.

Lord Henry will die before then.

A world without him in it was suddenly too much to bear. I felt shaken to the core.

Maybe there was a way to stop it. A way to warn him.

Phoebus was buzzing around making sure everything was in order. At least he wasn't taking notice of me. No one was. I could slip out easily in all of the hustle and bustle and no one would even realize I was gone. Harris, I'd overheard some servants saying, had left suddenly for London on some family emergency and wouldn't be back until the morning. One less person skulking around made it easier for me.

The roads were pretty straightforward. If I made a left at the bottom of the lane I could follow the same road all the way to Oxwich. It was still early enough that I could disappear and be back before sunset.

The small pouch of coins was tucked into the breeches I wore under my dress just in case I needed money. When I had tried to hand it back to Lord Henry he'd refused. Maybe he realized that I was destitute and at any moment his parents' kindness to me would run dry and I'd be turfed out with nothing. I was grateful to have it.

The only person in the barn was the young groom Jamie. Everyone else had been sent on various errands to prepare for the ball. It was easy to convince Jamie that I needed to take Angus out for a bit and without question he tacked him up for me and I was on my way.

I left at a leisurely pace to start with, and then I hurried along, anxious to put as much distance between me and the Dormer House as possible. It wasn't like I was a prisoner, but I didn't think they'd take too kindly to me taking one of their horses to Oxwich without asking. Everyone had their opinion of what I was: a whore, a thief, a simpleton. Even Lord Henry. I wasn't sure what he thought of me.

A naive girl—well, he'd told me that much. A charlatan? I had kind of jumped his bones.

When I got to Oxwich I stabled Angus at the Good Intent, as it was closest to the apothecary and I was worried about tying him up on the street. I wasn't sure how I'd explain to the earl that I'd not only taken one of his horses, but had it stolen. As far as anyone was concerned I was just going out for a ride.

Half running, half walking, I made it to the apothecary and then realized I didn't know what to do next. When would Miss Crabtree come? Or worse, what if she'd already come? Should I ask? Maybe I could get a cup of tea across the street while I waited.

The little tea room felt very much like a ladies-who-lunch kind of place. It was predominantly done up in pastel colors with paintings of flowers or food still lifes on the walls. All of the current occupants were well-to-do women sitting in groups of threes or fours gossiping about fashions and scandals. Obviously the news of Lord Henry's engagement was a hot topic, as more than two tables made some mention or another of it. One woman, in a hushed tone, revealed that the match had been made because the earl's fortune was in jeopardy. Another spoke about the fact that Jane was technically Lord Henry's first cousin, although not by blood, as the countess was only his stepmother.

It was difficult to stay focused on looking out for Miss Crabtree because my attention was continuously being drawn into the gossip vortex. Then a rotund pig-nosed girl started to say that she'd heard that Lord Henry wasn't even the legitimate heir to the earldom. She'd heard it directly from a ladies' maid to the countess.

I felt a strong desire to jump to his defense, but movement across the street at the apothecary caught my attention. An old lady dressed in black had just left and was already making her way down the busy road.

Shit. Panicked, I reached for my change purse. How much did a cup of tea cost? I had no idea. Soon Miss Crabtree would be out of sight completely and my only chance lost. My hands shook as I tried to pull out some coins from the little purse. I slammed down a shilling and made a dash for the door.

"Excuse me, miss?" the waitress called out but I was already out the door and dodging through people, horses and dogs.

My heart thumped in my chest like it was trying to hammer its way out completely. Where had she gone? There was a humming in my ears as I searched through the crowd for the woman in black. Frantic now, I raced up the street in the direction I'd seen her go moments ago. People stopped to look at me. I supposed I was making a spectacle of myself—a tall woman running alarmingly fast. I was sure I would soon be the talk of the town. Something caught my arm and I was yanked back and fell hard into Harris the creepy coach driver.

"What have we here?" His breath smelt of sour milk and rot. "A little far from home, are we?"

Busted.

The adrenaline coursing through my body made it difficult to feel my lips enough to speak. I hadn't accounted for the possibility of running into anyone I might know.

"I just had an errand to run." The ringing in my ears grew louder.

"An errand? Really, what kind of errand?"

"I had to return a book for Lord Henry. We bought it the other day but he decided not to keep it." *Oops, I forgot to bring it with me.*

"Without an escort? You on your own? Where's this parcel you speak of?" He searched me up and down for the parcel.

"I've already returned it."

"Then why are you in such a hurry? I've never seen a lass run like that unless she's being chased, and usually that's because she's gone and done somethin' she shouldna been doing in the first place. I wonder what milord would say t'your story? In fact, I think he'd be none too pleased to know you'd come on your own."

"Well, why don't you ask him? And why are *you* here anyway? Aren't you supposed to be in London on a 'family emergency'?"

Something passed across his face. Perhaps there was something going on that he wished to keep private.

"Ah, a smart little lass, are ye? I think you've got quite a few little secrets of your own." His eyes scanned my whole body. Was he coming on to me? Or was he the one who'd left the note under my door? Creepy on so many levels.

"So why were ye runnin'?" Clearly he was not going to let this go. He struggled to get some sort of leverage over me.

"I was going to check on the horse. I didn't want them feeding him too much before I headed back." This was thin but the best I could come up with in a pinch.

"I see, well, the Good Intent is the other direction." He pointed the way I'd just come from and watched closely for my reaction.

"How did—? I guess I must have gotten myself turned around." So he'd been spying on me. With a quick jerk I pulled my arm from his sweaty grasp, spun around and headed back the way I'd just come from. Chills rose up my spine. How long had he been following me?

He continued to watch as I made my way through the crowd.

All of this for nothing.

I'd taken a huge risk coming here and now I was no better off than before. My eyes started to sting and I swallowed hard, determined not to cry. What would Harris say to Lord Henry? Or worse, the earl and countess? How could I explain coming here on my own? What if the earl was angry and decided to throw me out? I felt the small purse of money in the hem of my breeches. At least I could survive for a short time.

I was so deep in thought that I smacked right into a woman coming out of a shop. She started to lose her footing and I reached out and caught her before she fell. Her body felt frail under all those layers of clothing. Once I managed to get her safely on her feet her white eyes met mine and I almost lost my balance.

Miss Crabtree.

Chapter 20

The Wayfarer

"You should watch where you are going. I know your troubles seem grave but if you lose sight of your path you really may have trouble following it." She wasn't scolding, simply stating fact.

"I'm so sorry I bumped into you." At the same time I was so relieved to see her I wanted to throw my arms around her frail little body and hug her.

"I should think relieved is more what you should be. Heaven knows I am." No wonder people thought she was crazy. She had a way of speaking your mind and knowing your thoughts that gave me the chills.

"How do you do that? How do you know so much about me?"

"Well, I may not see but I am a good listener. But let's not talk here, dear. Soon that dog that's been following you will come looking. Why don't we go somewhere more private?" She took my arm and led me down a narrow alleyway, away from the crowds beginning to take notice of us.

For a blind woman she was incredibly quick. She was continuously clucking with her mouth and I wasn't sure if it was some sort of nervous tic or just sheer excitement. Within minutes she led me through a complex route to the back door of what seemed to be a large three-story townhouse. At first I thought maybe she worked in this house, as the entrance we used was clearly meant for the staff. Just before we came to the stairs, a butler dressed up in his long coat tails joined us from the kitchen.

"Good afternoon, madame." He bowed respectfully.

"Ah, George, would you be a dear and have Annabel bring some tea to the parlor?" she said, hardly even pausing before heading up the stairs.

"Certainly, madame," he called after us.

When we came through a narrow door at the top of the staircase we walked into the main floor of the house.

"Is this your house?" I found it hard to mask my surprise.

"It's where I live for now. So yes, I suppose it's mine."

She led me to a beautiful little room with light pink walls and gold-trimmed woodwork, sort of a small version of the main sitting room in the Dormer House. The fireplace was done in carved marble. The corner window was rounded and there was a little table with two chairs tucked perfectly into that space. From there you could see the street below. It was much quieter than the main street but still had a fair bit of traffic, mostly horses and the odd carriage clunking along the cobbled street below.

As soon as we took a seat Annabel walked in with a tray of tea and biscuits. My stomach instantly started to rumble as I hadn't thought to eat before setting off. Annabel was just a girl of maybe sixteen with dark hair and a petite figure. In this time she was probably considered scrawny. Once she was completely out of earshot Miss Crabtree turned her unsettling white eyes on me again.

"So you're in a bit of a pickle." She cut straight to the chase.

I wasn't sure how to respond. Could she be trusted? My instincts told me yes but still I decided to err on the side of caution.

"Tell me why you say that," I said while I prepared my tea.

"Are we going to beat around the bush then? Are you not the one seeking me out?" She poured milk into her own tea.

She had a point. I didn't exactly have oodles of time to waste and this woman was as sharp as a tack.

"I'm still trying to make sense of everything that's happened to me these last few days. Where do I even start?"

"Start at the beginning." She stirred milk into her tea and then looked to me.

"Well, one second I was on a bicycle and the next I was…"

"No, we'll get to that. What do you know about your family?"

"Oh." I had no idea how any of that was relevant, but decided to appease the old woman whose help I was desperate for. "My father was from Northern California and my mother was from here, actually, and…"

"I see." She seemed to be making some sort of mental calculation. "That's where it starts, then. You are a rare breed, Miss Emma. Not many can do what you can. Your mother would have been the carrier, as it is always passed from the matriarch." She seemed to be mumbling to herself now. "Did she have sisters?"

"What? What was passed on to me?" I felt completely lost.

"You have no idea, do you? Is this the first time this has happened to you?"

"Yes. What do you mean, first time? What is *this*?"

"My dear, you are a Wayfarer." Her sightless eyes lit up like she was delivering good news. "Didn't your mother ever tell you?"

"A what? What does that even mean?" My hand had stopped stirring my tea and hovered frozen above it.

"It's what we—and by we, I mean a very small group of us—call someone who has the ability to go from place to place unhindered by any fourth-dimensional boundaries. That, my dear, is a Wayfarer.

You may know of it by other names, perhaps."

I took an extra moment to allow her words to soak in. A time traveler? That was ridiculous.

"How would my mother have known?" My mother had always told me I was special, but didn't every mother say that to their children? Surely something this big would have fallen out of the realm of 'special' and been classified in the 'extraordinary' category. If my mother had known, then wouldn't she have felt the need to pass on this little tidbit?

"She would have been one too, along with any sisters she might have had. What was her family name?"

"Farrar was her maiden name." Now I was trying to remember if she'd talked about any family. I vaguely remembered talk of a sister. If my mother had been a Wayfarer herself, how come she had never traveled? Or had she? "How could you possibly even know this?" Who was this woman? Was she one herself?

"When I told you I couldn't see but I could listen, that is what I do." Miss Crabtree took a sip of tea and pursed her lips, as it was still too hot to drink. "When a bat flies through the air at night searching for food, he uses his ears to guide him because he does not see. He hears the vibrations which tells him where things are."

"Is that what you were doing in the alleyway? With that clucking?" I interrupted. It was the most unusual thing I'd ever seen.

"Oh, that." She chuckled. "A dear friend showed me that little trick. It's called echolocation. Yes, that's certainly part of it, but for me, people also give off a certain vibration which tells me a great deal about them."

"Okay, but what makes you think I'm a Wayfarer or whatever you called it?"

"Well, I have met a few others and all of you have had the same type of vibration. Think of it like meeting a hummingbird. If you could hear his wings beating you would be able to differentiate him from a pigeon, for instance, if you knew what to listen for." Miss Crabtree had moved on to the biscuits and I followed suit. I didn't feel I could take in anything more on an empty stomach. "You have a very unique vibration that sounds like a high-pitched hum, so strong that I can feel it when I stand close enough." She brushed away crumbs from her lips as she spoke.

"Really?" Weren't old people notoriously hard of hearing? Mind you, in the realm of time travel, maybe super-hearing wasn't completely out there. "So if you know so much about what I am, do you also know how I get back?" The clock above the mantel was ticking loudly and I was reminded that I didn't have too much more time. I needed to get back to Dormer House soon before someone noticed I had disappeared.

Miss Crabtree's lips were still pursed in thought as she considered my question. "I'm not sure, dear. Emily used to think it had something to do with big bouts of energy. She called it electricity, I believe, but that was just one of the triggers." She jumped out of her chair like an agile kitten suddenly in search of something. "That reminds me."

"Emily? Who is she? Is she a friend of yours?"

Now Miss Crabtree blushed a bit.

"We were a little more than friends, dear." She winked at me. "In her time she said it was quite common, you know, and that women were even allowed to marry each other. Can you believe that?" She gave a little schoolgirl giggle and seemed more surprised by that little detail than the fact that her lover was a time traveler, or Wayfarer, as she called it. She found what she was looking for and brought the small wooden box over to our table. It was only marginally smaller than a shoe box, with a sturdy-looking lock on the front.

"So you know someone else from my time?" Same-sex marriage

was a fairly recent event in the future I was from.

My mind was being blown in so many directions. It was liberating to finally be able to talk to someone about this. I hardly paid attention as Miss Crabtree pulled a small key from a chain around her neck and opened the lock.

"Ah, that's what I wanted." She spoke softly to herself as she reached in and took out some sort of black crystal on a thin leather string. "Here, you'll need this." She placed the necklace in front of me.

"What kind of stone is this?" I touched the rough edges of the crystal carefully, half expecting it to have special powers.

"It's called tourmaline. Emily thought that the weak electric current that flows through it suppresses electromagnetic fields around you. She felt that it protected Wayfarers against the negative effects of travel and even helped them have more control of it." Her white eyes were misty.

"Thank you," I said.

Miss Crabtree pulled a small notebook out of the box and slid it over towards me.

"What's this?"

"It was Emily's last journal. You may find some of the answers you're looking for in there." I could tell this was difficult for her. "You can't keep it, but you may borrow it," she added quickly.

"I'll make sure I get it back to you. What about Emily? Where is she? Did she make it back?"

"Emily Crouch was her name when I met her." Miss Crabtree's expression changed. "I don't know for sure if she made it back, but I do know that when I met her it was not her first time traveling."

"You mean she'd done it more than once?" It had never occurred to me that someone would want to go through this experience multiple times. "Could she control it?"

"She was convinced there was a way. Maybe her journal would shed some light on that for you. She always wrote things down for me because my memory isn't what it used to be."

"How long was she stuck here?" The first prickle of alarm echoed through my body, giving me the beginning of a headache.

Miss Crabtree got very quiet and I figured that she was having difficulty remembering.

"Eight months and three days." A single tear welled up in her right eye but it never fell, it just hovered there threatening to fall.

Eight months? I could be here for that long? Panic wound its way through me like an intrusive vine and the tips of my fingers lost all circulation. The tick-tock of the clock felt loud and menacing, like it was aware of its own irony. How could I survive here for that long? It would be only a matter of time before I found myself homeless.

"Don't go getting your knickers in a knot." Miss Crabtree had gone back to her bluntness. "When she traveled before it only lasted days or weeks. She wanted to stay here. She was convinced she could control it. That's why she always wore that stone around her neck." She made a motion toward the crystal she'd just given me. "She might have succeeded if things had turned out differently."

What things?

I wanted to press the old woman but the wind seemed to have left her sails and she looked tired and run down.

"Be very careful to leave things just as you found them." She seemed quite concerned with the last bit and looked at me with a serious expression. "*Just* as you found them."

Her tone had become much more serious, but I wanted to hear more about Emily. Obviously she would have come from roughly the same time period as I had.

"What happened to Emily?" I watched a cloud gather over Miss Crabtree and realized that I had probably asked the wrong question.

Once again my curiosity got ahead of my brain. It was kind of like asking a woman who couldn't have children if she planned to have them.

"She tried to change things." Her white eyes were unblinking.

This sounded rather ominous. I didn't want to seem insensitive, so I simply waited for Miss Crabtree to come out of her melancholy.

"She told me you would seek me out, you know."

Her words sent icy fingers down my spine. How could that even be possible? I certainly didn't know an Emily Crouch. Did she know me?

Chapter 21

The Tunnel

Leaving Miss Crabtree's townhouse, I hurried along the busy road towards the Good Intent. I hadn't expected to stay so long but Miss Crabtree had insisted I have some food before setting off. Now street vendors were backing up their booths for the day and patrons hurried along the winding roads and alleys for supper.

Guests would already be arriving soon for the ball and it would be difficult to slip in unnoticed, especially looking the way I did. Every time I turned a corner I dreaded being spotted by Harris, who might very well be combing the town for me.

Angus whinnied so loud when he heard my voice it was embarrassing. In reality, I was glad to see him too. Being around horses was always the best way to alleviate my stress. After my mom died I used to spend hours in my favorite horse's stall, letting his soothing energy calm my emotions. I would sit in the corner of Shorty's box stall while he chewed his hay, then search my pockets for hidden treats or remnants of sugar cubes.

After paying the groom, I mounted and trotted off towards Dormer House. The sun was getting low but it was nowhere near dark yet. It was that perfect time of summer when days felt like they went on forever. We kept a steady trot, occasionally breaking into a canter when we hit an open stretch.

Everything Miss Crabtree had said played over in my mind. The term Wayfarer, she explained, meant traveler. I was a time traveler. Suddenly the gravity of that hit me. It was simultaneously exciting and terrifying. Figuring out how to navigate this knowledge would be tricky. She knew it was possible to get back, but she wasn't entirely sure how. Once she'd done a little more digging she promised to get back to me. At least that was something and it was comforting to finally have someone know my secret. A small weight had been lifted off my shoulders. Living a lie as I had for the last few days was becoming more and more difficult. I'd struggled to keep my story straight, especially with the countess watching my every move and questioning my every response.

Emily, it turned out, was an English woman from the North. She was from the same area my mother was from, just outside Manchester. Miss Crabtree wouldn't elaborate on what had happened to her and I didn't want to press the issue. At least not yet. How this woman could possibly know anything about me was unclear. Miss Crabtree seemed foggy about the whole thing. Maybe I'd find something useful in the journal.

When I got to the last bend just before Dormer House would come into view, I took a deep breath and tried to prepare myself for the coming evening. With any luck, I could make a brief appearance and then lock myself in my room for the rest of the night and devour Emily's journal. Lord Henry would no doubt be busy enjoying Jane's unrelenting adoration, a fact that made me feel ill, even if I had no right to it. Maybe I could score a nice bottle of red to keep me company. That thought cheered me only slightly.

The stable was quiet, with most of the staff assisting up at the house. Jamie, the stable boy, was left alone to tend to the horses. He hopped up as soon as Angus and I walked through the big doors.

"Good evening, miss. We were quite worried about you, we were. Milord thought you might have been back ages ago. I was just about to come out looking for you. Glad to see you safely returned though."

He was already setting about untacking Angus, who was quite anxious to get to the grain in his stall. So Lord Henry knew I'd gone out. I hoped that wouldn't come back to bite me.

"He was none too pleased that I let you leave on your own, miss."

"I'm sorry." I really didn't want this poor boy in trouble because of me. "I didn't mean to worry anybody. I must have lost track of time." I could only hope that few people were aware of my absence. "Tell me, Jamie, do you know a more discreet way into the house? I don't want to walk through the front door looking like this."

He took in my outfit. "No, you certainly don't. I can take you through the tunnels. We're not meant to use them except in emergencies, but maybe this once." He finished up with Angus and put him away for the night. "This way, miss." He grabbed one of the lanterns hanging by the door and lit it. "Hold this a minute, will ya, miss?" He handed the lantern to me so that he could shift a bale of hay over to the side and pull up a trap door from the floor. "Please don't tell anyone I showed you this. No one's meant to use it. That's what me da tells me."

"I won't."

He looked at me skeptically.

"Cross my heart and hope to die."

This seemed to satisfy him, as only children could be satisfied by pinky swears or heartfelt promises of death.

He took the lantern from me and started down a short, narrow, steep staircase. The temperature immediately dropped several degrees. It smelled musty from a prolonged absence of fresh air, like walking into a crypt, and I wondered if this was really a good idea.

Just when I made it to the bottom several black-winged things went flying by in a panic to get past me and I couldn't help but scream.

"Shhhhh." Jamie was eager to keep me quiet. "They're just bats, miss, they needn't hurt you."

I had to will my feet to move. I hated bats. I tried not to imagine what other lovely creatures lurked here in the dark. Rats. Spiders.

"I'll walk you all the way, but you must keep quiet. I'd lose my hide if we get caught."

"Where does this lead?" I wondered how safe this tunnel was.

"The basement of the house where they have the wine cellars. Most of the servants no longer live down there—they live on the west side of the property, other than Mr. Phoebus and Miss Barnsby. The kitchens are also there, so you'll have to be careful."

"Oh. Okay." This was starting to sound riskier than just walking through the front door.

The only light came from the lantern. The ceiling was low and if I reached up I could touch it without even straining, but instead I hunched low to avoid it or anything possibly dangling from it. Halfway through I tripped over something on the ground and skidded across the stone floor. My right knee was left raw from the unforgiving surface.

"Are you all right, miss?" Jamie scurried back and helped me to my feet.

The light from Jamie's lantern revealed a beautiful silver candelabra discarded carelessly on the ground. It was the kind of candlestick that belonged not in a tunnel like this but on a dining table.

"What's that doing here?" I asked.

"I dunno, miss. That's a curious place to find such a thing." He made no move to pick it up and I assumed that he had no way of turning it in without revealing where he'd found it. So we simply pressed on.

When we reached the house Jamie shoved the door open just a crack to make sure the coast was clear. My heart started thumping in my chest like an erratic drumbeat. My nerves were already frayed from my encounter with creepy Harris, the last thing I wanted was to get caught in here.

"The servants' stairs are down the hall to the right. The kitchen is the other way so you should be fine. Go up three flights and that should bring you to your floor," he whispered and turned to double-time it back to the barn.

"Thank you," I whispered after him, but he was already halfway gone.

The door was opened only enough for me to squeeze through. On tiptoes I stepped as quietly and as quickly as my boots would allow. When I was just about to turn a corner, I heard feet scuffing along the ground and men's hushed voices. In a panic, I swallowed my heart and did a three-sixty to see where I could possibly hide. Just beyond the tunnel door I found a small dark alcove. I tucked into the darkest corner of it and tried hard to steady my breathing. I sounded like Darth Vader and considered covering my face with the sleeve of my shirt.

"You mustn't raise any suspicion when you break away from the hunt," the first man said.

"Of course, and what about the billet straps? Will they be cut just enough on the saddle?" the second man asked.

"Yes, that will be taken care of," the first man replied impatiently.

"Does he usually check his tack before mounting?"

"No, I've never seen him. Oh, and lead him as far away as possible from where the others will be hunting. No one must see you together."

"I will take every precaution."

"See you in two days. Godspeed." One of the men walked past my hiding place. I was too afraid to try to peek. Whatever they were plotting was not intended for anyone else's ears.

I heard the heavy door for the tunnel open and then close. Hopefully Jamie had already made it to the other side. The other man went back the way I was supposed to be headed, so I stayed hidden for a while until I was sure he was long gone. Who on earth were they talking about? My mind raced as I tried to piece together the fragments of conversation I'd overheard. Brushing the dust off my clothes, I headed for the servants' staircase. Just as I was about to turn the handle, the door opened and there stood Miss Barnsby with a shocked expression.

"What on earth are you doing down here? Where've you been all day? The countess asked me several times already if I'd helped you dress for the ball." She was already red in the face and I was afraid she'd soon spontaneously combust.

"I came down looking for you." The lie came out easily—it was becoming an occupational hazard of mine.

"Well, let's get you upstairs, the party's nearly half over."

For the first time missing half a party felt like a relief.

Chapter 22

The Ball

With one last check in the long mirror, I was ready to go. It felt like I was attending a costume party. The dress Isobel had lent me was a light blue tarlatane evening gown with a delicate lace and ribbon trim. The neckline swooped down in an oval shape, just barely kissing my shoulders. The arms puffed out before tapering just above my elbow. It was a relief to have the scar on my upper arm covered completely, as I continued to wear a small bandage over it.

The many petticoats I wore underneath—I counted six in total—made me look like I had an enormous behind. Apparently the cage petticoat had yet to grace nineteenth-century fashion. If I was stuck here much longer I would need to introduce that accessory sooner than later.

"I'm not sure why Miss Isobel was so insistent you wear this one. It's been out of fashion for quite some time." Miss Barnsby finished the buttons in the back as she spoke. "But nonetheless, it looks far better on you than it ever did on her." I couldn't tell if she meant that as a compliment to me or an insult to Isobel. Or was her purpose to make me feel insecure about wearing a dress no longer in fashion? Little did she know, I was not and had never been a fashion victim.

If it fit and was comfortable I liked it.

Miss Barnsby took special care to do my hair, putting it up with matching blue ribbon and delicate flowers. Most woman would be wearing some form of headdress, but she felt that because my hair was so 'beautiful'—her word, not mine—it was best to do as little as possible. Perhaps I was winning her over slowly but surely.

The shoes were a little less comfortable. I imagined tripping and falling flat on my face à la Jennifer Lawrence at the Oscars. With this giant dress it was going to be difficult to simply blend in with the furniture.

In a flutter of nerves like I was going to prom, I was escorted by Miss Barnsby down the hall only as far as the staircase. I was forced to do the last leg on my own like Cinderella arriving late to the ball.

Not at all the effect I was going for.

Lord Henry, who had been deep in conversation with a small party including Jane, stopped mid-sentence to stare. Jane had to crane her neck in an awkward way to see what had grabbed her fiancé's attention so suddenly. A part of me relished the attention from Lord Henry and the turmoil it spurred in his betrothed.

Once at the bottom I pretended to be looking for a friend. Of course I had none, but it gave me an excuse to walk into another room. Isobel noticed me from the other side of the room and glided over with a drink in hand and a smile on her face.

What a relief!

"You look incredible, Miss Clayton." She used my surname now out of politeness.

"And you too, Lady Drake." I hoped I got that one right. All these people went by so many names it was impossible to keep track. Especially someone like me, where names went in one ear and out the other. I made a mental note to work on that this evening.

"Shall we take a stroll?" She took my arm and guided me towards the great room where people seemed to be gathering. "And maybe you can tell me where you were all day," she said in a confidential manner. Did everyone in the house know I'd left? This was a very slippery slope.

"Just went out for a ride and got a bit lost. They really should have better signposts."

Disappointment filled Isobel's eyes. "I thought you might have more interesting gossip to share. Like maybe a secret rendezvous?" She winked at me. Did she know? Had Harris come back and reported where I'd gone? Maybe I should confess that I'd gone to Oxwich? "You know, with a certain lieutenant?" Isobel arched an eyebrow at me, trying to coax a confession.

Relief washed over me. "Nope, nothing that exciting."

"It's been terribly boring here without you. Mother has been dreadful with all her preparations." She continued to lead me from room to room with her arm tucked into mine. "So I've been scoping out the guests for anyone who looks remotely interesting, but with little luck, I'm afraid."

Many inquisitive eyes followed our every move, but Isobel hardly noticed. She was on a mission of her own and I was so relieved for the distraction that I gladly played along. When we heard the forced, clipped laughter of the countess from the next room we changed course and strolled in the other direction. The dancing had started in the large drawing room and Isobel dragged me with newfound purpose. The dance master stood near the orchestra, directing the night's entertainment.

We were not standing long before a young man with short dark hair parted down the middle and meticulously combed came to us and asked Isobel to dance. A familiar waltz by Franz Schubert brought the dance floor to life as couples stepped and spun in constant rotation. I watched and took it all in. All the men were dressed in a similar way—black tail coats of fine fabric, with white or black waistcoats and pressed white shirts under that. Most of the men wore white neckties, but a few wore black. With every room bursting with guests, it was difficult to calculate how many people were here.

Once this song ended another started and Isobel was already dancing with a new partner. This time, it was a faster-paced number—a polka, I heard one woman say, where couples took only two short steps before twirling. I was mesmerized by the quick footwork. A couple of men looked my way, but no one dared to approach. Instinctively, I took a whiff of my underarms just to make sure the foul odor I was smelling was in fact not coming from my own body. Without the luxury of deodorant sticks, I had been dousing myself in lavender or rose oils. In a pinch I'd resorted to a handful of potpourri rubbed over my entire body.

My feet started to ache and I thought it might be a good time to make my escape. Then I caught sight of Lord Henry and Jane dancing together. Call it morbid curiosity, but as much as I felt torn up watching it, I couldn't take my eyes off of them. They were gracefully dancing together. Of course Jane would be a good dancer, she'd no doubt been taught to play piano as well. Lord Henry looked like he was having a good time. This tore at my heart. Jane, of course, was all smiles and giggles.

On one of their turns around the room he caught sight of me staring and I immediately looked away. I felt humiliated getting caught. At this point, I decided that I'd had enough and turned to make my way quietly to my room, but before I could Isobel was beside me, panting and asking me why I hadn't been dancing.

"I'm fine. I'm not really very good." Not exactly true—I was great at Zumba, but I doubted if that counted.

Lord Henry was walking in our direction. Now, I felt desperate to leave but Isobel was still holding my arm. Short of wrenching it from her grasp I was stuck. Isobel's eyes twinkled mischievously when she saw her brother.

"Darling brother, do dance with Miss Clayton—no one has asked her and she is so lovely this evening." She gave Lord Henry her best puppy-dog eyes. He in turn gave her a 'meddling sister' sigh.

"Oh, don't worry. When I said I wasn't very good I meant it." I silently cursed Isobel for putting us both on the spot. I could tell that Lord Henry was hesitant. He scanned the room for someone. *Probably for Jane.*

"Miss Emma, would you do me the honor?" He reached his hand out to me. Isobel grinned at him like a proud sister.

"You know, you are not allowed to refuse, Emma, otherwise you might be found guilty of an incivility," she teased.

When I took Lord Henry's hand all the hairs on my arms came to life and stood to attention. Even through our gloved hands, the heat from his body transferred immediately to mine and my cheeks started to burn. It would be a gross understatement to say only a few eyes were on us. So many eyes burrowed holes in my back that I felt like Swiss cheese. There was no turning back now, not without causing some sort of fuss or embarrassment.

"I'll try not to step on your toes." My feeble attempt at a joke. It was a comfort to hear him laugh. These were the first words we had spoken to each other since that night in the stables. Both of us tried hard to act as if nothing had ever passed between us.

"I heard you were out for a ride today?" he said by way of conversation.

"Yep." I wasn't ready to offer anything more. Maybe Harris had already told him, so I thought the less said the better.

"Need I remind you of the dangers of traveling unaccompanied?" There was only a hint of reprimand in his tone.

"No, you need not," I said with a smile.

He simply studied me for a second before nodding.

He put one arm around my waist and the other continued holding my hand, waiting for the orchestra to start. He had not a crease in his suit, nor a stray hair out of place as I allowed my eyes a quick scan of Lord Henry. Impeccable as always. *He can't possibly be human.*

Tiny explosions went off in my belly. It must be nerves, I thought to myself.

When was the last time I'd danced with a man?

Neither of us were sure where to look. It felt like an eternity before the music finally started. We made our way around the entire ballroom in constant rotation, dancing to the Sussex Waltz. It was probably used in hundreds of movies depicting a nineteenth-century ball. When our eyes finally met they locked and everything else in the room faded away. He was a great leader. I hadn't been this close to him since our kiss and though it had been just the once, my body was ringing with the memory of it.

Since the news of his engagement I had been careful to avoid him, perhaps more out of my own sense of self-preservation. But somehow being apart even for that short time had only increased my desire for him now. The intensity of longing was palpable. Was he feeling the same way? His fingers pressed into the skin on my back and desire for him welled up inside me like butterflies, fluttering, begging to be released. His eyes grazed mine, conveying far more than either of us were prepared to say. The sensuality of this hidden exchange felt charged and dangerous, like the blowing winds before a storm, unpredictable. What was wrong with me? Where was the off switch? A fire had been lit here and the more I tried to put it out the more I seemed to fan the flames. A battle raged inside me. Around and around we turned. Until, all of a sudden, bony fingers dug into my arm, breaking our embrace, and I found myself staring into the eyes of the devil herself: the countess.

"May I cut in?" It wasn't a question but a threat.

Lord Henry was quick to pull on his mask of indifference. I made a less fluid attempt to do the same. Lieutenant Walker came to my rescue and saved me the embarrassment of walking off the dance floor myself. He took my hand.

"Would you do me the honor, Miss Clayton?" His perfectly chiseled features gave even Batman a run for his money.

"Thank you, Lieutenant. So nice to see you again." It was genuinely a relief to see him. Someone had to bring me back to reality. We began gracefully dancing around the room. "I haven't seen you all night." I struggled to switch gears.

"No, I've only just arrived, and by the looks of it just at the right time." The medals hanging off his red uniform were blinding and made tiny clanking sounds as we spun.

"Yes, it would appear so." His charms would make most women swoon. Sadly, not this one.

"Poor Henry," he said and we both looked to his friend dancing stiffly with the devil. "That woman has always had a bee in her bonnet."

I laughed out loud at his candid remark about the countess, relieved that I wasn't the only one who found her unbearable.

"She's always been so jealous of Henry's mother that she's taken it out on him his whole life."

Out of the corner of my eye I could see Lord Henry watching us. "Oh?" It had never occurred to me that the woman had any feelings, let alone jealousy.

"Yes, it's well known that the earl married for love the first time around and when she died, part of him did too. He needed a woman to raise his son and keep his house. He couldn't have chosen a more wretched one for the job if you ask me." He laughed under his breath.

I didn't feel like laughing. It sounded so sad for everyone.

Suddenly I understood why the countess was so sour. Bitter even. How sad to be with a man who could never love you the way you wanted to be loved.

When the waltz ended another began, and the lieutenant asked if we could continue dancing. He was very entertaining and loved to tell story after story about his adventures overseas and all his strange encounters. It always felt like he was on and for now I found it a perfect distraction.

And so it went for the next three dances until I was sweating profusely and desperate for something to drink. The lieutenant left me in search of refreshments for us.

"Oh, Emma, I saw you dancing with the lieutenant," Isobel gushed as she joined me. Her arm slid through mine and she steered me to the nearest chair.

"Were you spying on me?" I teased.

"Oh, yes, I think half the people in this room remarked what a handsome couple you make." She was being sincere.

Just at that moment Lord Henry walked past us and Isobel called out to him.

"Wouldn't you agree, Henry? Didn't Miss Emma and the lieutenant make a handsome couple?" She was so thrilled to be playing matchmaker.

"I wouldn't have noticed." He said this looking at me. "Excuse me." He bowed his head and left the room abruptly.

"Well, I wonder what spoiled his pudding," she said in a reproachful tone. Her recovery was quick though when a short lank-haired boy approached us. He seemed hesitant and almost looked as if he would turn tail and run.

"Umm… Lady Isobel? Would you be so kind as to accept the next dance with me?" He looked more relieved once he'd finally managed to say the words.

"I'd be honored, Lord Waverly." With a quick glance back at me she mouthed the words, 'I'll be back,' before she disappeared into the next room.

Within moments the lieutenant had returned and handed me a glass of wine. "Would you like to get some air, Miss Clayton?" He held out one white-gloved hand to me.

"Sure, why not?" I got up with his help and allowed him to steer me out towards the patio.

"It's a beautiful summer evening, isn't it?" He didn't wait for an answer. "These are the very stars I love to gaze upon when I'm at sea."

"Ah…" I wasn't really sure what else to say. "Have you spent a lot of time at sea?" I tried to make conversation. He ignored my question and kept to his train of thought.

"You know what my favorite thing about being on a ship is, Miss Clayton?" He stared up at the stars. "It's the sense of adventure." He said this like it was some great reveal. "Going to far-off lands and taking in the uncivilized customs and cultures is a most fruitful venture."

"I'm sure it is." Political correctness was not the lieutenant's strong suit.

"I've had so much excitement in my life thus far, yet…" He turned to me and took my hands in his. "I still long to find the right person to share those stories with."

"I imagine that would be nice for you." I felt a bit awkward and not entirely sure where this was going. "You know, if you found the right person."

He had a handsome face but when I looked into his eyes, it was like staring into a giant abyss. An empty space. He pulled my hand to his lips and kissed it, letting his lips linger that extra moment.

Something caught my eye and we both looked over towards the house. Lord Henry stood in the doorway watching us. With lightning reflexes, I pulled my hands away from the lieutenant's as quickly as if I'd been burnt on a stove. Lord Henry turned and walked through the milling crowd.

"Looks like we've been discovered." Lieutenant Walker said with mock sheepishness.

What did he mean by that? Discovered doing what? What could Lord Henry possibly have seen or overheard? I started to feel guilty, but had I done anything wrong?

"Should we go back in?" I said, glad for the interruption. "I think Isobel will be looking for me."

"Yes, of course." He didn't seem thrilled to have to share me, but appeared determined to act the perfect gentleman. "I suppose I have monopolized you long enough." He forced a smile and led me back into the house.

Isobel came to my rescue.

"Lieutenant, may I just steal my friend for a moment? We have much to discuss." She giggled and without waiting for a response snatched me right out of his arm. "Oh, do tell me what the lieutenant said to you, Emma."

She reminded me so much of April. Never missed a thing and always wanted the download right away. April's greatest pet peeve was to hear you say, 'Oh, remind me to tell you what happened.' She needed it right away. She was the kind of person who made small holes in the wrapping paper so that she could see what her presents were at Christmas.

"Not much. He talked about being on ships and his faraway adventures. That's pretty much it." I played it down for fear she might cause some sort of scene if I mentioned that he was looking to settle down.

"But I saw him take your hands, Emma."

Busted. Had everyone noticed that?

"Oh, right. Did he?" I was never very good at acting but maybe ignorance could work too.

"Are you really immune to flirtation, Emma? I wager the lieutenant will call on you again."

I really hoped not but she looked so excited by the prospect that I didn't want to crush her spirit.

"How about you? How was your dance with Lord…" I could not remember what he was lord of—they all sort of sounded the same at this point.

"Lord Waverly." She looked underwhelmed. "Father would never approve a match like that. His family is on the verge of financial ruin, everyone knows it. Poor boy. It was pleasant enough."

"Do you wish William was here?" I whispered in a confidential tone.

"Who?" Isobel's nose scrunched up when she was confused or didn't like something.

"You know, from the other night?" I was still trying to be subtle.

"Don't be silly, Emma, he'd never fit in here." Her expression smoothed.

It was amazing how quickly she changed her tune. Just then a waiter passed with a tray of wine glasses and her attention shifted to grabbing us each a glass. I had to remember to pace myself or I'd be spending the rest of the night with my face in my chamber pot.

Another suitor arrived to ask Isobel to dance and she handed me her glass before she was whisked away.

Once out of sight, I decided to beat a quick retreat before the lieutenant descended on me again. I started for the stairs until I noticed the countess holding court with a small group. The last person I wanted to be noticed by was her. Instead, I slipped out the front door, which had been opened to allow some fresh air to dilute the overpowering smell of sweaty bodies.

Both wine glasses still in hand, I made my way to the stables. Carriages lined the road away from the house, waiting to whisk the partygoers home. Dull chitter-chatter could be heard as the drivers gossiped amongst themselves and shared sips of whiskey from small flasks. Tall oil lamps lit the path. They looked like the old-fashioned version of tikki lamps. The music from the orchestra could be heard echoing through the rolling hills outside.

It was a relief to breathe in the fresh air. My head was swimming from all the fumes. I wasn't sure what was worse, the strong body odors or the even stronger perfumes people wore to mask them.

One lamp burned at the far end of the stable. As soon as I walked in the horses stirred and some of them whinnied. A couple of them even kicked at their stall doors, thinking that it was time to be fed.

"Shhhhh, it's not breakfast," I said to no horse in particular.

Angus heard my voice and called out.

"Okay, okay, I'm coming." I grabbed a blanket with gold stitching from the tack room, balancing the two wine glasses in one hand, and then slid into his stall. This big puffy dress was not ideal, so I managed to wiggle out of a few petticoats before sinking down on the blanket to drink my wine. The straw made it comfortable. Angus poked around and searched me for treats, but sadly I hadn't thought to bring any. My only thoughts had been of escape.

The wine was a delicious treat and the first glass, which was more like a goblet, was done in no time. My idea was to wait out the party and sneak in just as the guests were leaving. However, after two large glasses of wine my will to move had lessened. When my eyes closed I told myself I would just rest for a second.

I woke with a start.

Right away I knew the energy in the barn had changed because the horses seemed anxious. Angus' ears were perked forward and he looked straight out his stall door. I didn't move a muscle but tried hard to listen for any indication someone had come in. It would be a bit awkward to be found in a horse stall, so I decided to wait it out. It was still dark outside and I could hear the faint music from the ballroom going strong so at least I knew I couldn't have fallen asleep for too long.

Then feet shuffled on the stone floors. My heart started to race. The footsteps faded into the tack room. A second set of footsteps came scurrying into the barn.

"Hurry up. Someone's coming," the second man said in a stage whisper.

"The blanket's not here. I don't know which one." The first man matched the urgency. "How do I know which one to cut?"

"It's the black one." I could sense the exasperation in his voice. The second man clearly felt like his friend was the village idiot.

"Most of them are black."

The second set of footsteps approached and disappeared into the tack room. "He said the one with gold stitching. Look, try this one and quick."

I could hear a slight rubbing sound.

"Let's go. Through the tunnel." Two sets of footprints scurried over to the trap door. I heard the wooden door shut and knew they were using the bat tunnel.

What on earth had happened? Obviously I had taken the blanket in question, but what was it meant for?

Before I could think about it I heard another set of footsteps in the barn. The horses did not seem alarmed this time. One of them kicked his stall, but I couldn't tell which one. The movements of the new person sounded bigger than a boy's, so I doubted it was Jamie checking on the horses.

"Shhh, boy," said the man in a soft voice.

Lord Henry.

I closed my eyes and mentally cursed my bad luck.

Chapter 23

A Fight

Angus, convinced that another horse was getting treats, started banging on his stall door until the whole thing vibrated, threatening to come off its hinges altogether. I tried to distract him, but he was having none of it. His hooves simply pounded with more enthusiasm until Lord Henry walked over.

"Angus, what's wrong with you?" he said in a voice reserved for animals.

When I heard the familiar sound of a hand on the latch of the stall door, I buried my head in my arms, wishing myself invisible.

"Oh, Angus, what a fine petticoat you have. I hope you've behaved like a perfect gentleman."

My body convulsed with laughter. It was such an unexpected joke that it was impossible not to. When I looked up Lord Henry met my gaze with a quizzical expression. He was the image of pure innocence.

"Am I interrupting something?" He looked at the empty wine glass and I laughed a little harder.

"As a matter of fact, you are. You've ruined my perfectly good hiding spot." I started to get up and smooth out my dress.

"Well, I suppose you've also ruined mine. So that makes us even."

He looked a little drunk. It was refreshing to see him a little more relaxed.

"You? What on earth are you hiding from?"

"Life, responsibility, the watchful eyes of my stepmother…" He paused. "You." He chuckled a little to himself. "Take your pick." He slid Angus' door open so that I could come out, but stood blocking my path.

"Why are you trying to hide from me? I mean, I get your stepmother, but…" I felt a familiar flutter in my belly as I squeezed past him.

He took the blanket and wine glasses from me and put them in the tack room. When he walked back out he had composed himself completely, all humor gone. "It would be imprudent for us to be discovered here alone. Let me escort you back to the house."

My heart sank. I wanted to stretch out this moment alone with him as long as I could because I knew it could easily be our last. Clearly he didn't feel the same way and that stung.

"I can take myself when I'm ready." I turned away, tired of being told what to do and not feeling in control of anything. Nothing seemed clear anymore. Didn't I have a fiancé myself? Why was I so conflicted about Lord Henry? Why did I find myself searching for him every time I walked into a room? Why did it feel so good being near him?

"You know I can't allow you to go wandering alone in the dark," he said as if it were written in some etiquette handbook. It wouldn't surprise me at all if it was. There seemed to be rules for everything.

"Of course you can. I'm a big girl. I'm not afraid of the dark." Now I just wanted to be left alone.

"I would worry for your safety." He wasn't used to being challenged, certainly not by a woman. His arms were crossed and he looked like he was sizing me up in case he needed to throw me over his shoulder and haul me away.

"Well, you don't need to. What could possibly happen to me here? I am more than capable of taking care of myself."

"I don't doubt that for a moment," he agreed under his breath, "yet I feel obligated to…"

"Obligation." It felt like a bad word. I wanted to lash out at him. The effects of the wine were making it hard to stop myself. "I am not your obligation. Where's Jane, anyway?"

He closed his eyes like I'd just sucker-punched him. "She's gone back to the inn with her family." I'd clearly hit a nerve.

"Oh," I said, but it was a loaded 'oh' and he knew it too.

"That's not fair," he said, bristling with indignation. "Must I explain myself, Miss Emma? Well, here it is. Our estate will more than double with this union and it has been in the works for quite some time. Jane's fortune will secure our family's future and therefore it is my duty to marry. Believe me when I say it was not my doing." He shook his head. "I didn't know that it was going to be so soon."

He watched me, waiting for me to respond or maybe agree, but I did nothing.

"I tried to explain to you," he continued.

"After you kissed me?" I shouldn't have said that but I couldn't stop myself. He didn't owe me an explanation. Nothing had really happened between us, but why did it hurt anyway?

"*You* kissed *me*!" His face was red and his eyes full of accusation.

"Oh, is that how you see it? You weren't exactly putting up much of a fight." I'd really thought it was mutual, but maybe I had misread him.

His mouth was open, ready to say something, but he shut it as he must have thought better of it. The truth was, it didn't really matter. I was just looking for someone to take my frustration out on. There was another emotion I was feeling, but I couldn't quite put my finger on it.

"Well, you seemed to have bounced back with some ease. Perhaps you are overly generous with your affections." He had reined in his anger.

"What is that supposed to mean?" It came out slow and clear.

"Are we all so interchangeable to you, Miss Clayton?" He was now pacing in front of me. His manner was cutting, delivered with such indifference it felt like a knife through my heart.

"What are you implying?" Part of me wanted him to say the words but at the same time I willed him not to go there.

"Well, if I'd not interrupted your inappropriate conduct with the lieutenant, who knows how far that might have gone as well."

"How dare you! And you consider yourself such a gentleman! You're the one who's to be married. I'm surprised you even took the time to notice," I spat back.

"How could I not?" He was shouting at me now. "Everyone else in the ballroom did too. A woman of good breeding wouldn't dream of being so demonstrative with her affections with someone she hardly knew."

My body physically recoiled from his comment. *Good breeding?* Was I some sort of animal now?

"What, are you jealous?" I matched his tone. I was not about to show a chink in my armor. *Sticks and stones may break my bones, but names will never hurt me,* I urged myself to believe. But his words did hurt and I hated him for it.

"Jealous?" He said this like it was the most absurd idea.

"Yes," I hissed through gritted teeth. "Jealous!" I took a step closer to him and stood defiantly with my arms crossed and my heels in the ground. If I could have looked down on him it would have been great, but he was much taller than I was so I settled for raising my chin.

"How could I be? The lieutenant is far less discriminating with the women he chooses for companionship. He's the type of man who boasts about the numbers of whorehouses he's visited throughout his travels."

My head burst into flames and I lashed out and slapped Lord Henry hard across the face.

I'd never in my life done that before. The sound was not quite as satisfying as it was in the movies. My palm stung from the impact. His face contorted sideways from the blow.

Neither of us saw that coming.

He grabbed both my wrists to stop me from belting him again. My face must have signaled that that was my intention. All I saw was red. He had to hold me tight because I was struggling so much to free myself. I was enraged at being compared to a whore and I wanted to inflict as much pain on him as he had just inflicted on me.

An eye for an eye.

The more I struggled the harder he held me. He gripped with enough force that I thought my wrists would snap. At some point tears started falling from my eyes and when I looked up at my assailant he loosened his grasp only a little, but something else had changed too.

His lips came down on mine with such force that I thought it might have split my bottom lip open. His tongue forced in. The metallic taste in my mouth combined with the salt of my tears and the wine on our breath.

I wanted to slug him again, but my body had turned traitor. Instead, it gave up the fight and responded to him. Our kissing was turbulent at first, with increasing urgency. We were like starving animals having food for the first time. Nipping, tasting, exploring. It reminded me of those French movie romances when a physical fight always led to some passionate liaison. My brain was flashing 'danger, danger' but my body was acting independently.

When his grip loosened on my arms I swung them around his neck. My fingers ran through his thick dark hair, pulling him closer. We couldn't even come up for air. He picked me up so that my legs were straddling his torso. One hand slipped under my bum and the other tangled in my hair, and we staggered back, pinning me against Angus' stall door.

His lips pulled away to kiss along my neck, sending goosebumps traveling over my entire body. I squeezed him between my thighs and he gasped. His fingers pressed and dug into my flesh as if he wanted to rip me apart. When his body pressed harder against mine it released a flutter deep in my belly.

He pulled back only inches from my face to search my expression. His eyes were such a clear, ocean blue and I wanted to lose myself in them. In him. I held his gaze and then dove in. Opening myself to him completely.

He lowered me down but kept me pinned against the stall. Both hands now cupped my face. The metal latch dug into my back but I didn't care. I bit his lower lip with my teeth and his whole body shuddered. He in turn nipped me at the base of my neck and I almost buckled at the knees. His lips brushed along my exposed shoulder until I wanted to burst.

"I do not understand the power you wield over me, but I cannot get you out of my head." His voice was husky and breathless in my ear, sending a fresh new wave of butterflies fluttering under my skin. A smile tugged at my lips.

"You have a strange way of showing it," I said in a playful tone.

"The English never show their true feelings, as you've been kind enough to point out," he said, matching my tone. "We prefer to keep things bottled up."

Ah, so he had been listening to my little rant. "Glad to see you're breaking the mold."

"You've made it impossible for me to do otherwise. Any woman brave enough to smack me upside the head is worth a second look."

I raised my hand to threaten another beating and he stole a kiss.

"I don't usually like to use violence as foreplay, but in your case…"

He looked at me curiously. "I am in awe of your use of the English language, Miss Emma." He laughed.

His fingers traced along my collarbone and my nipples tightened in response. I pulled his lips back to mine and our kissing became more urgent. The evidence of his desire pressed into my abdomen. Never had I wanted anyone the way I wanted this man. Not just in a physical sense, which at the moment was blinding, but in every way. I wanted to know him and love him and be loved by him. It was like a light had been turned on in my very core and now I could no longer imagine living in darkness. Not ever again.

My hand slid down his back, tracing the muscles through his shirt. I was desperate to feel his skin. There was far too much fabric between us which needed to be peeled away. With a tug I pulled his shirt from his pants so I could feel the heat of his flesh in my palms.

He looked down at me, his eyes full of questions.

Are we going to do this?

Both of us knew there'd be no turning back. I reached for his hand and brought it to my breast in answer. His eyes closed for a moment, as if this was the first time he'd touched a woman's body. Maybe it was. Without another thought he lifted me with ease and carried me to the tack room. There was an old leather couch on the far side and we crashed down on that, never breaking our kiss. How he found his way so flawlessly in the dark was a mystery. I had given up long ago caring what was becoming of Isobel's delicate blue dress. Miss Barnsby would most likely have a heart attack when she saw the state of it.

Henry lowered his body on mine until I felt the full weight of him. He reached around and loosened the snaps that held the top part of the dress snug against my chest. Finally I could breathe a little better. He leaned onto his side and with my breast in his palm my nipple hardened under his touch. His mouth brushed across my breast, the sensation sending a steady wave of pleasure through my body. Encouraged by my reaction he continued until I felt on the verge of orgasm.

An overwhelming desire to feel his skin on mine took hold of me. In a series of quick tugs I undid his cravat and popped the buttons off his shirt, revealing his perfect chest. For a man who had probably never seen the inside of a gym, nor done an ounce of physical labor, he was toned and muscular. I ran my hand over the lean contours of his body as he watched.

"Stand up." His voice was almost hoarse, but full of command. "I want to see you." By now our eyes had adjusted to the darkness. Moon slivers cut through the curtains overhead like the faint strokes of a paintbrush.

He helped me up and undid my dress. Heedless of the wrath of Miss Barnsby, he let it fall to the ground. Moving behind me he traced a line from my shoulders to my neck with his lips leaving a small trail of wet kisses. A pleasant shiver ran through my body as he got to work on the corset. When that fell to the ground he looked at my body through the loose-fitting shift. My nipples brushed against the delicate fabric. With one small tug the shift fell like a thin curtain down to my ankles. My skin filled with goosebumps and tingled with the warm summer air.

I reveled in the way he watched me. Instead of feeling vulnerable, as I always did even in front of a mirror, I felt strong and empowered. There was no judgment in his eyes, only love and acceptance. Next he slid down my drawers and stockings, tossing them aside like used-up paper.

Reaching out to him, I felt his excitement through his clothes. He held his breath for a moment before letting it out in shallow bursts. Now it was his turn to watch as I undressed him, letting his clothes join mine on the floor, a tangled mess. We were past the point of no return. Whatever might come, I wanted to bend to his will and have him bend to mine. I took him in my hand, feeling the extent of his need. When he couldn't stand it anymore, he picked me up and laid me down on the sofa. He kissed me all the way down to my navel, nipping and tasting indiscriminately. My body and mind surrendered to him completely. He paused at the small tattoo of a bird in flight just below my navel.

"What's this?" He traced it with his finger.

"Oh, it's just a silly little thing I did when I was young." I hadn't thought about how to explain it. Miss Barnsby had noticed it but she'd pretended not to see it. Isobel had certainly been intrigued with it, but I couldn't imagine what Henry would make of it.

"It's beautiful." He traced the bird with his tongue. The whole time he snuck smoldering glances at me as my body contorted to his pleasure like a puppet masterfully manipulated by invisible strings. He smiled when I shivered involuntarily. My body had never responded like this to anyone. With him I felt like a different Emma, the Emma I was supposed to be. The woman inside me had finally woken up. There was no telling what Henry had unleashed.

When the teasing became unbearable he spread my legs and tasted me. My head fell back and I quivered under his tongue. He stopped only when he felt my whole body convulse, my hips rising up to him. The power of my orgasm was so strong that I struggled to catch my breath. But before I had recovered completely he slid into me.

Our eyes locked onto each other. How could this feel so right? But it did. Our bodies, our souls joined, speaking without a need for words. With each movement he went deeper inside me. Sweat dripped off his body and fell onto mine. We moved with more and more urgency, our breathing becoming ragged. I raised my pelvis to join his and urge him to enter further inside me and he did just that until both of us were on the edge and then convulsing together. We took shallow breaths, slippery with sweat. He collapsed onto me and kissed me until I stopped shaking.

We lay intertwined for some time before either us had the strength to move or even speak. He stayed inside me, still trembling himself. Naked and tired and blissful, cocooned within the safety of his body, I felt like I'd finally come to life.

His lips moved to my ear.

"I have desired you from the very core of my being and beyond all reason since first we met." He looked at me with all seriousness. "I love the way you see the world and the pleasure you seem to take in living in it. It's not like anything I've ever encountered."

I kissed him slowly and then pulled away. "I've never felt anything like this before." My feelings for Ben all this time had never come close to what I was feeling at this moment with Henry. How had I accepted such a mediocre amount of love and caring and passion? Maybe I hadn't felt I deserved better? Perhaps a small part of me was always the child abandoned. The death of a mother and the neglect of a father had always left me wanting but never getting. Here I was getting the love that should always have been mine in the first place, one without fear or compromise.

"Nor I." He traced the outline of my lips with his finger. "I was driven mad with jealousy when I saw you with John. I am dreadfully sorry for my appalling behavior." We both laughed with the memory of our heated argument.

"You're forgiven."

He laid his head on my shoulder, his arm wrapped around my waist possessively. His heartbeat struggled to go back to a normal rhythm. When I felt the rise and fall of his steady breath I knew he had fallen asleep and I stroked his hair, getting as much comfort from the gesture as I hoped I was giving.

I wasn't sure if I imagined the sound of shuffling feet or the blurred outline of someone in the doorway, but I felt another presence in the room besides us. Sometimes when you tried too hard to listen all you could hear was a ringing that seemed to get louder the harder you strained to hear. I gave Henry a small nudge at first, and then as I became more sure of it, I startled him awake. When he lifted his head we both heard the unmistakable sound of feet running from the stable.

Who had seen us? And what had they seen? Most importantly, who would they tell?

Chapter 24

A Little Bird Told Me

When I finally made it to my own bed I had trouble falling asleep. At any moment I imagined that the countess might barge in and drag me out by my hair, yelling, "You wretched whore!" We'd snuck back into the house undetected, but someone had seen us at the stables. My mind was a flurry of activity which I struggled to rein in. My wildest fantasies and worst fears battled to take center stage. What would happen now?

My body tingled and ached. I felt bruised. It was pleasure verging on pain. Our affections had been a little rougher than I was aware of at the time.

My lips were swollen and my face felt chafed. Maybe tomorrow would be a good day to stay in bed. The idea of Miss Barnsby's face when she saw the state of the dress made me feel slightly ill. Or even the state of me. Surely she'd notice the bruising by morning. Her clucks of disapproval already echoed in my head.

That would be nothing compared to the scrutiny I would receive from the countess. Maybe I could come up with a story of falling out of bed. And then there would be Isobel. She'd be on tenterhooks to find out where I'd ended up and what had happened with Lieutenant Walker.

The skies were already the dull gray of early morning. It had to be about five am. The robins had started to chirp and soon the house would wake up too.

When oblivion finally did arrive it was short-lived. Some people were talking outside my bedroom door but I couldn't make out who the voices belonged to until the unmistakable exuberance of Miss Barnsby shooed them off before knocking on my door. She no longer waited for me to answer. The door was flung open with no apology and she started to buzz about her business. There were a few dramatic intakes of breath, which told me she'd seen the blue dress. Maybe if I just kept my eyes closed and pretended to be asleep I wouldn't have to meet her gaze and I could delay the inevitable scrutiny.

"You'll need to get up, Miss Clayton, the countess desires an audience with you," she said in a tone as if I'd been called to the principal's office. There was almost pity in her voice.

Almost.

"Don't want to keep her waiting." She'd gone back to her singsong voice like I was a child in her charge.

"Ahhhhh!" was pretty much all I could manage.

"Are you unwell, child?"

"Maybe." I knew I wasn't ready to face the day. The thought of it made me feel quite ill.

"Nothing a little fresh air won't cure." She flung the windows open and set about putting out my clothes. "Now, I've got about five minutes to make you presentable."

Might as well get it over with. I flung my feet out of bed, already feeling a little stiff. Miss Barnsby gasped when she looked up at me.

"Oh, this will take more time than I expected."

My hair was a complete tangle of knots.

With gritted teeth I endured her rough brushing. I winced during the worst of it. She took a cloth to some of my bruises, thinking they were just dirty marks, and when she realized they wouldn't come off she clucked judgmentally.

"What have you gone and done to yourself? Were you wrestling with an ox last night? Your wee arms are covered in bruises."

I had to fight back the urge to smile when I thought of Henry, certainly as stubborn as an ox. My heart gave a little flutter as I imagined him fast asleep somewhere in the house.

Both of us had been on edge sneaking through the house last night like common thieves. Neither of us had wanted to be separated but it was impossible to take any more risks. He'd said he would find the right time to speak with his father. Did he mean to call off the wedding? What would that mean for us? Was that what I wanted him to do? Did no wedding mean no hunt tomorrow? That meant that his life would be saved. It also meant that he would be free to choose.

My heart started to beat faster at the thought that maybe we could be together. Ben's face flashed before my eyes and I felt ashamed for my betrayal. Where did my feelings for him fit into all of this? What about getting back to my real life?

"Miss Clayton, did you hear a word I've said?" Miss Barnsby snapped at me.

She was pulling the corset strings a little tighter than I thought necessary. Perhaps she was as uneasy about my meeting with the countess as I was.

"Um, I'm so sorry. I guess I must be in a bit of a daze."

"The countess will see you in the library. Shall I have some tea sent to you there?"

"Sure. I mean, yes, please." Her thoughtful suggestion caught me off guard. Was I finally starting to win her over? The idea of being alone with the countess snapped me back to the moment. "Is anyone else awake?"

"Everyone, miss. It's already half past two."

"Oooh. All right then." I'd had no idea that I'd slept that long. It had felt like minutes, not hours. "Thank you, Miss Barnsby. I really appreciate all you've done for me."

She struggled to meet my eyes, like I'd somehow made her uncomfortable. Perhaps she was not used to being thanked.

With a pit in my stomach, I made my way down the winding staircase. What was I going to say? Did the countess know what had happened between Henry and I? This felt more like walking to the guillotine. Standing at the door to the library, I took a few deep breaths to calm my nerves. The clock on the landing chimed three times. And then I caught sight of Henry coming down the steps. I willed him to look my way but he didn't. Instead he went directly into his father's study, his expression grave. Maybe he had reservations—or worse, regrets—about last night. Should I feel regrets?

It was amazing how all evidence of last night's party had already been erased. If the scent of Lord Henry did not still permeate my own flesh, I'd question if it had happened at all. Every article of furniture had been placed back in its usual spot like it had never been moved.

As I walked in, the countess was sipping her tea. She seemed in surprisingly good spirits. The sweet smell of cigar smoke still lingered in the library despite the open windows. For the first time the countess looked at me and smiled—not a particularly warm smile, as I doubted her face could actually accomplish such a feat. I looked behind me to make sure she wasn't smiling at someone else, but there was no one else in the room. Maybe I would be spared the lashings after all.

"Good morning, Miss Clayton, or should I say good afternoon?" Was she trying to be funny?

"Oh, right. Yeah, I guess I did oversleep a little." My palms instantly started to sweat. It felt like I'd just walked into a job interview.

"No matter. I trust you enjoyed yourself last night?"

"You put on a very nice party, thank you." Maybe she wanted to start fresh and get off on the right foot.

"Yes, I did, didn't I?" She took another sip of tea and gestured for me to sit. "It appears Lieutenant Walker was quite taken with you. He was most distressed when he was unable to bid you farewell."

Or maybe not.

Thoughts of the guillotine flooded my mind, or a noose dangling from a lonely perch.

"Umm, yes. I was suddenly not feeling well, so I took myself to bed early."

"Of course." She watched me intently, her steel-gray eyes unblinking.

One of the footmen came in carrying a tray with my tea and some biscuits. It was a relief to have something to focus my attention on. The countess had a way of making me want to crawl out of my skin and be absorbed into the furniture.

"It wouldn't surprise me at all if the lieutenant came calling again," she said with a smile that carried enough warmth to freeze a shallow puddle.

I wasn't sure where she was going with this.

After a sizable pause, the countess pursed her lips. "I have made inquiries about your mother's family, the Farrars, but it seems I have reached an impasse. The Farrars we tracked down in the North have only four young sons and no daughters."

I swallowed a huge gulp of tea and scorched the top of my throat. I'd never imagined she would go through the trouble.

"They have no knowledge of an Eileen Farrar either."

"Oh. Well, my mother never spoke of her family. I'm sorry I'm not much help." I could tell that she knew I was stalling. She had the right family, only a few generations too early.

"I heard you went to Oxwich yesterday. Did you have someone to visit there?" The noose was tightening.

"Ah, no, I just needed to return something."

Harris hadn't wasted any time.

"Return something?"

"A book. When I was there a few days ago I bought a book and realized that I didn't want it after all." Sweat started dripping down my cleavage. What was this, the Spanish Inquisition?

"With what money did you make such a purchase, dear?"

"Well," I started, "Henry—I mean Lord Henry—kindly lent me some." Had I said too much? Could I faint suddenly? Didn't women always swoon during this time?

"I see." She took a long breath. "And in what manner were you to repay him for this kindness?" She asked it innocently, but her words were like nails on a chalkboard.

She knew. She was toying with me like a cat played with a mouse before they ate it. She enjoyed watching me squirm. She knew there was no family to be found. She knew I hadn't gone to bed early. It wouldn't surprise me if she knew about Miss Crabtree, but what she didn't know was what I was hiding.

There was a knock at the door and the earl, Lord Henry and another middle-aged gentleman walked in. The gentleman was dressed in nice clothes, but somehow they hung on his body more loosely than they should. Kind of like a teenage boy trying to wear his father's suit. He was clean-shaven but did not hold himself with the confidence of the men he stood next to.

"Ahhh, the men have arrived." The countess stood to greet them. "Good afternoon, gentlemen," she said in a cheery tone like we were all dear friends. The earl looked a little grim himself and made no effort to match his wife's enthusiasm.

"Let's have a seat." The earl motioned for the stranger to sit. The man, never taking his eyes off me, sat in the armchair directly across from mine.

Lord Henry did not budge from where he'd entered the room. He stood, unsure where to look, and my heart started to race. I swallowed the growing lump in my throat. What was this all about? Was this the man who'd seen us in the stable? Were they going to confront us about what we'd done?

"This is Mr. Jacob," the earl said as he cleared his throat and directed this introduction to me alone. "He rode here about an hour ago in search of his wife, who had gone missing several days ago." He spoke slowly, as one might do with a small child.

"I'm sorry for you, Mr. Jacob," I said with genuine concern, but I was really unclear why they were telling me this. Did they think I knew this woman? I could feel Lord Henry's eyes on me now but I didn't meet them. Everyone looked to each other as if I'd done something unexpected.

The earl shifted in his seat and I could tell he struggled with how to proceed.

"Well, Miss Emma, the woman he searches for…" Sweat dripped from his brow and he pulled a handkerchief from his pocket to dab at it with the shaky hands of a drinker. This small gesture reminded me of my father.

Outside I could hear the clatter of hooves as a single horse trotted up the lane.

"Is Emma Jacob. Her maiden name is Clayton."

My neck almost snapped out of joint, I turned so quickly to look from the earl to this stranger.

"What?" None of this made any sense. Was this a joke?

"Mrs. Marc Jacob, this is your husband." The earl pointed

towards the stranger, or should I say imposter.

"You've made a mistake. I'm not married. I don't know this man!" Bile rose in my throat and I swallowed it down. I looked to Lord Henry, who wore a mask of distrust and confusion. Did he believe this?

"I know this may come as a shock to you, as you have yet to regain your memory, but this man has the proper documents and appears to be who he says he is. There are a few more matters that might help us with this little mystery though."

He summoned Phoebus over. I hadn't noticed Phoebus lurking in the corner this whole time. He had an uncanny way of blending in with the tapestries.

Phoebus walked over to the earl with a satisfied grin on his face, like the kid in class responsible for bringing down the popular kid. In his gnarled little clutches he held my purse, the one I had lost in the accident. My mouth fell open as if the hinges holding it there had broken.

"Apparently, this was found on your person during the accident. Harris was kind enough to retrieve it and keep it safe. Can you explain why you were in possession of a bag with the name Marc Jacob on it?"

"Yes, I can." This all seemed so ridiculous. "Marc Jacob is a designer who makes handbags and…"

The earl looked furious. "Young lady, I do not tolerate lies." His face had gone many shades of red and for a moment I feared he might have a heart attack. "You stole your husband's bag and made off like a thief." Phoebus gave me a knowing look that said, 'I knew her to be a thief.' "And now this ridiculous charade of yours must come to an end."

My mouth opened and closed like a fish out of water.

"Mr. Jacob has a marriage certificate in his possession that shows him to be wed to an Emma Clayton."

The stranger pulled a paper from the inside of his jacket and handed it to me to look at.

With shaky hands I took the document that was passed my way but didn't look at it.

"Is that not your own signature?" the earl continued with forced patience.

When I glanced down, sure enough, in black ink, there was my familiar signature next to the space marked 'spouse'.

How is this even possible?

Panic rose in my throat. Signed on the bottom line by a witness named William White, the document looked legitimate, but I knew it was a lie. Who was this William White? The name itself stirred something in the very back of my memory, but not enough to recall it completely. It was more of a vague awareness that the name rang a bell.

I wasn't sure how long I sat studying the document, but the earl broke the silence first.

"Mr. Jacob tells us a story of an unsatisfied wife who thought she deserved a higher station and who left in the night with his few valuables."

"That's ridiculous! I've never laid eyes on this man." This was absurd.

"He also describes a marking of a bird just below your navel. Is this correct?" the earl said in a tone of disgust.

How could they know? Miss Barnsby? My eyes turned again to Lord Henry who reluctantly met them. Inside, I could tell he was seething like he'd been duped.

"This is bullshit!" I was being framed and I could hardly contain my anger.

"I'd watch your tongue, Emma." The stranger finally spoke. His voice was gruff, like someone who chain-smoked. “You’ve made a fool of yourself and of me and imposed enough on the kindness of the earl and countess.”

“Henry!” My own voice sounded hoarse to my own ears. He looked just about to leave the room and clearly leave me to this man. He leveled a cold stare on me. “You can’t believe any of this? They are lies.”

“How do you know this man is not who he says he is? He seems to have knowledge that only a husband should have.” There was judgment in his tone, not just directed at me but at himself too. “There is nothing I can do. You are this man’s property. Perhaps we should all rejoice that we have been able to reunite you with your family.” His tone of indifference was cutting.

“I can prove I’m not his. Let me see the purse.” I wasn’t sure my driver’s license would help me overall, but at least it might prove that I wasn’t this moron’s wife, which seemed more important than anything.

The earl handed it over. With numb hands I searched inside but found nothing. “What happened to my things?”

Lord Henry glanced at the earl, who looked to the countess as she shrugged her shoulders.

“Madame, the bag came to us as you see it now. Perhaps you sold all the valuables,” the earl said with no small amount of condescension.

“This purse is hardly big enough to hold any valuables, but I had a few things in here,” I snapped at the earl. How could I possibly describe what was in there? My ID, an iPhone and British pounds from 2015. I was dead in the water.

“So you don’t deny taking the bag?” the earl thundered back.

“Isn’t it convenient that your memory has suddenly appeared? You are a liar, Miss Jacob, and have tainted our family with enough scandal. You should gather up your few things and leave Dormer House immediately," the countess said with satisfaction. Unlike the earl, she was enjoying every second of this exchange. I imagined that she would relive these moments on many occasions in the company of her peers, herself expertly painted as the victim and graciously accepting their kind words of condolence.

The earl stood to show that the discussion was over.

With tears pooled in my eyes, it felt like I was looking through tiny kaleidoscopes, tapestries and furniture bleeding into each other. How could I possibly explain? Only hours ago I'd felt safe and loved. How quickly everything had shifted. Even Lord Henry had turned his back on me. My heart sank when it occurred to me that he now regretted what had happened between us. It felt like I would burst with sadness and betrayal.

The imposter stood and took my arm in a rough hold.

"You heard the countess, Emma," he said in a stern voice.

"Do not touch me, sir." I felt like a snake ready to strike. I stomped out of the room. Maybe I could run away to Miss Crabtree. She knew the truth and maybe she could help me.

Chapter 25

More Time

I took the stairs two at a time. Tears pooled in my eyes, making it difficult to see. All I wanted was to get away. Everything around me was unraveling and I needed to pull myself together and make a plan. There was no time to deal with a broken heart. I would have to save that for another day.

How could I have been so naive? Who had put this Marc Jacob up to it? What could he possibly have to gain? Harris knew something. If he was the one who had had my purse all along he must have done something with my things. While it would hardly prove my innocence, it would show that I wasn't that man's wife. If only I could see Henry alone. Maybe I could convince him of the truth. That would have its own implications, but at least I wouldn't be turned over to someone like cattle. I was no one's property.

With the door shut tight behind me I scanned the room for anything that I would need to take. Sadly, nothing was mine. Even the clothes on my back were Isobel's. My leggings and long top were laid out for me on my bed. Miss Barnsby must have set them out there when she found out I'd be leaving. Maybe she'd played a part in this whole charade. After all, how would they know about my tattoo? Maybe the walls did talk, as the countess had told me days ago.

With shaky hands I tore at my dress and stripped it off. I felt practically naked now in my own clothes. Perhaps that was what they wanted, for me to feel naked and vulnerable. The sleeve of my top had been mended where it had torn. On the dresser lay the rough stone necklace that Miss Crabtree had given me and I put it around my neck. I doubted it could do much for me, but it was a comfort to have it just the same.

My door knob rattled and Isobel snuck in. When she saw the state of me, she bounded over and gave me a hug. I collapsed in her embrace.

"I am terribly sad to see you leave. It has been so nice to feel as though I have a sister." She had tears in her eyes.

"Isobel, none of this is true, you must believe…"

"Shhh. I know." She cut me off and hugged me tighter. "There was commotion last night after most of the guests had left. Mother wanted to find Henry and of course no one could. She suspected he was with you."

She looked at me now with a questioning look. I nodded with a guilty expression. There was no point in lying now. She smiled at me like she respected me even more.

"Watching the two of you dance, it was obvious there was something there. Poor Lieutenant Walker never had a chance." Isobel was easily distracted when she was telling a story. "Well, anyway, when I was on my way up to bed I did overhear Mother plotting. She said something about teaching you a lesson or some such thing." She looked at me apologetically.

"You have to tell Henry."

"Oh, Emma." Now she burst into real tears. "I cannot meddle. If my mother knew she'd have me married off to the most hideous creature she could find and that would be the ruin of me. I'm sorry."

My heart sank at her words. She looked genuinely terrified. She acted as if her troubles would be so much worse than mine. I even felt sorry for her for a minute.

"But Isobel, you can't just let that man take me away. This isn't right."

"I wish I were strong like you, Emma, but I'm not." Her tears dried almost as quickly as they had started. "I only came to tell you how much you will be missed and to give you this." Out of her cleavage she pulled out a sealed note. "I intercepted it this morning. I don't think Mamma would have given it to you." She looked proud of herself for gaining one small victory over her mother.

"Thank you." Not quite the help I had hoped for. I wasn't sure how a note would help, but I took it.

"Here, take this." She swung her shawl over my shoulders. "You can't be expected to go out looking like that." She looked mortified that I was to leave with so little clothing. "I also had Miss Barnsby pack up that dress I gave you."

"Oh, thank you." We both knew that I'd have little opportunity to wear it wherever I was going.

"I will miss you. Life will be so dull hanging about with Jane while all the men go out on the hunt tomorrow."

Of course, the hunt. Lord Henry's life was in danger.

"Please do something for me, Isobel." Now I was pleading.

She nodded, intrigued by the note of mystery in my voice. She loved being part of some sort of drama.

"You have to convince your brother not to go on the hunt tomorrow." Even though he'd abandoned me in my time of need I couldn't bear the thought of him dying.

Her face fell. She must have been prepared for professions of love. "What, Edmund?" She looked confused.

"No, no. Henry." She was sweet but not always the sharpest tool in the shed.

"Why should he not go? It is in his honor." She looked at me with a puzzled expression. "He's a terrific hunter, Emma."

"I just don't have a good feeling about it. Promise me." How on earth did I explain?

"He would never heed such advice from a woman, and his sister, no less. I think I'd have better luck moving an ox." She laughed.

"Right." Again with the ox analogies. "It would mean a great deal to me if you tried."

She shrugged her shoulders in a noncommittal sort of way.

"Oh, and one last thing. Could you have a book delivered to a Miss Crabtree in Oxwich? I'll scribble her address down for you."

"Oxwich? What business do you have there?" She sounded intrigued.

"Isobel, I don't have time to get into that. Can you see that it gets there?" I didn't want to be so cryptic but I had little time.

"Very well." She was a little distracted with some commotion downstairs and I wasn't sure if she was listening.

I grabbed Emily's journal and started to wrap it in the parchment paper from the book store. Parting with it before I'd even had the chance to crack it open was torture but I knew how important it was to Miss Crabtree.

"I must go, Emma." She gave me a quick hug and took the book from my hand.

"Thank you."

She paused at the door before leaving. "I hope our paths cross again."

Then she left as quietly as she had entered. I knew I didn't have a lot of time. Now that I was a supposed thief they would be worried about things I might try to pilfer. I took the Brontë book with me for company but nothing else in the room was mine. The wheels in my head were working on overdrive trying to devise a plan. At the first opportunity I would run away. If I could break away on horseback I would do it and somehow find my way to Oxwich.

As I made my way down the stairs Lord Henry was making his way up. He avoided my eyes. The staircase was wide and just before we would come into view of anyone in the foyer I stopped him.

"You have to believe this is madness," I whispered but hated the desperate tone in my voice.

"Madame, I know nothing of the sort. I am clearly the most inept judge of character." His eyes were red and swollen. Had he been crying?

Unlikely.

"But Henry, that's a lie. You know me. I wish I had more time to explain but I don't. There are things I haven't told you but they are not these. Find out what Harris has done with my things. It won't explain anything but it will prove that I'm not this man's wife."

While he would never know what to make of my California driver's license, at least it might show him that there was another explanation.

"You are talking nonsense, Mrs. Jacob." He looked at me with cold eyes, all the love and tenderness from last night stripped away. It was shattering to see him look at me this way.

"Henry, is that you?" the countess called out from downstairs.

"Please, Henry, don't go on the hunt tomorrow. If you ever cared for me at all…" I tried to hold his arm so he couldn't walk away from me because he refused to meet my eyes.

"Henry, come down this minute." The earl cut in, sounding less than amused.

"I cared for a woman who does not exist." He jerked his arm away. "If you'll excuse me, I have a hunt to prepare for." And he continued up the stairs. Away from me. Away from his parents. This would be the last time I would see him and the thought almost made my knees buckle.

Chapter 26

The Letter

There was a small chestnut mare saddled and waiting for me in the front yard. She looked more like a mule than a proper horse. My plot for escape was doomed.

Just when I thought the day couldn't get any worse, Lieutenant Walker stormed out of the house carrying a small bouquet of flowers that swayed violently in his hand, the delicate petals like confetti on the path. He had obviously just learned of my apparent circumstances and had most likely been the one causing the commotion that had distracted Isobel. Men like that did not like to appear foolish.

I was too overwhelmed with my own dire circumstances to give his ego a second thought but it made matters worse to have an audience. His adoring looks from last night were now replaced with a scornful grimace.

How quickly my life had changed. It was not his rejection that tore a hole in my chest though. What role had Lord Henry played in this little plot? The earl wore his disapproval for everyone to see. How could any man know a woman's body if he'd not seen it first hand? That was the way they all thought. Lord Henry could hardly even look at me. Maybe I should have told him the truth about myself from the beginning. But how would that have gone? Now everything was lost. I was being dragged away against my will, Henry was going to die tomorrow and for all I knew so was I.

Flanked by the earl and Phoebus, the imposter Marc Jacob sat on his own mount, which looked like a show horse by comparison to the mule I would be riding. Phoebus smirked when he saw me standing at the top of the steps. A righteous smile was plastered on his face.

I considered making a run for it, but how far could I really get? And wouldn't that condemn me further? No, I would not give them the satisfaction. I was also done with pleading my case. With my head held high I made my way down the few steps towards the men making me a captive. My fingernails dug into my palms to distract me from the stinging in my eyes. I was determined not to cry. Not again. Instinctively I turned back towards the house and noticed the countess perched by one of the second-story windows watching her devious plan unfold like someone might watch the climax of their favorite show. *What goes around comes around,* I thought to myself.

"Thank you for your kind hospitality." I bowed slightly to the earl as I'd seen Isobel do whenever addressing someone above her station. With the use of a mounting block I got up in the saddle.

Mr. Jacob didn't trust me either as he kept hold of my mare's reins. Another setback in my plot to escape.

"Safe journey," the earl said before turning towards the house, clearly relieved to be done with the altercation.

I stared straight ahead until we were almost at the end of the drive where the house would soon disappear forever. Only then did I dare to turn back. There was movement in my old room—probably Miss Barnsby doing an inventory to make sure nothing else was missing—but no sign of Henry.

As we walked past the stables I allowed myself one last thought of him and our evening together before I set about the exhausting task of paying attention where we were going in case I ever found my way back.

After the second hour of riding we stopped briefly to give the horses a break. I hadn't uttered one word to my captor the entire time. He offered me some bread and cheese from his nasty-looking saddlebag which I refused with the smallest hand gesture. My stomach rumbled. For a moment I wondered if I was being ridiculous. However, it was unlikely I could keep anything down.

Mr. Jacob seemed more than happy not to have to engage in conversation with a woman and sat chewing with his mouth smacking open like a child who hadn't yet learned manners. He washed his meal down with what smelled like home-brewed whiskey. Moments later we were back on the move.

We hit a fork in the road and took a path that ran along a wide creek. I was grateful for the small landmark as up until that point it had been rolling hill after rolling hill and forest canopy after forest canopy, all looking indistinguishable from the other.

A creek was something different and we followed it for another forty-five minutes before turning off a path that led to a small wooden shack maybe slightly larger than our two-car garage back home in L.A. There was a small turnout ring for the horses next to a run-down hen hut where five chickens pecked at the dirt rhythmically like those golden Maneki-neko cats they sold in Chinatown who continuously waved one lazy arm.

The cottage had only one tiny window in the front, with a shutter to close it but no glass. It was a far cry from Dormer House.

So this is to be my prison.

How long would they try to keep me here? Until the wedding, maybe, or else until… my thoughts trailed off to Lord Henry's lifeless body lying at the base of the creek near the White Hart. I took two large gasps of air as his demise became more of a reality.

Mr. Jacob looked over at me as if noticing me for the first time. "Cheer up, little hen, it isn't that bad. I'm an easy man to keep." A lecherous grin revealed the extent of his tooth decay.

He took another long swig from his flask. I wasn't sure how many he must have gone through on the journey. With any luck he would simply pass out. In the meantime I got hold of my emotions and decided to play along.

"Oh, it's every bit as I imagined it," I said, flashing him a smile. He looked at me like I had suddenly grown another head. "Shall I fix us a meal, husband?"

This time he almost fell off his horse. During the ride I'd had a lot of time to think about tactics, and what better way to ward him off than by making him slightly afraid of me? What if he thought I was crazy?

He watched me tentatively, waiting for my head to spin around full circle.

I jumped off the little mule, whose name I'd learnt was Maybelle, and stalked over towards the shack. The strong musty smell of body odor, stale beer and general rot filled my nostrils when I stepped inside. Going from daylight to darkness, it took several seconds for my eyes to adjust and when they did the place left even more to be desired.

There was an unmade bed in the far corner, with only a wooden crate standing in as a makeshift night table. One oil lamp stood in the center of it, unlit. A dusty-looking terrier scampered my way, barely able to bark. He wheezed like an old man with emphysema. Poor thing. I bent down to pet his wiry coat. He could not be blamed for any of this. He had to be at least a hundred in dog years.

The kitchen consisted of a fireplace with a stone hearth and a wooden table for chopping and preparing. A large cauldron of boiling water hung in the center of the fireplace. It was already two-thirds empty. Three different-sized pots hung from nails in the wall above. Root vegetables lay scattered on the table, becoming limp.

Moments later, Mr. Jacob came in, barring the door behind him and locking it from the inside. The key, which hung from a ragged string, was placed around his neck and tucked into his shirt. Without a word he heaved his heavy saddlebag onto the only table and emptied some of its contents. There were cured meats, fresh cheese, a loaf of bread, a small bag of apples and even a bottle of the whiskey made at Dormer House.

"I'll just have some of this, love," he sneered at me. With an apple and some cheese in hand, he headed to one of the two chairs in the cottage.

"Sure." The way he leered at me made my skin crawl. I found the book I'd brought, my only possession, and went to sit by the single window.

The sun hung low, getting ready to make its final plunge. This was going to be a long night and I hoped that my friend wasn't going to get any funny ideas. It was bad enough to be abducted by this stranger, but I was still trying to figure out what he might have been promised for this little exchange.

I stared at the words on the page but nothing registered. The best I could do was pretend to read as my mind raced. How could Henry have allowed this to happen? Could this connection I'd thought we had be nothing more than a physical attraction? Men were pretty good at keeping those things separate. It felt much deeper than that for me. Had I been so credulous? I mentally reprimanded myself for it.

Now what? As a swell of panic started to take root I touched my heart to help stop it beating so quickly in my chest and felt the crunch of paper. In all the craziness of the afternoon, I'd forgotten the letter that Isobel had handed me earlier in the day. At the time, it had seemed so irrelevant as I'd had much bigger problems at hand, but now, all alone, I clung to it as some might cling to a Bible in their darkest hour. It could only be from one person. The only friend I had. Miss Crabtree.

Chapter 27

Claustrophobic

All night the words in Miss Crabtree's letter kept fluttering around in my head. The part that troubled me the most was the last line of the letter when she said to take care, because she feared I was in danger.

How could she have known what the countess was plotting against me? If it wasn't this, could there be some other danger she was referring to? Either way, I doubted if I'd ever know.

At least Mr. Jacob had left me alone. He snored soundly from the safe distance of his bed. After consuming an entire flask of some foul-smelling liquid, he'd passed out. Dangled over the side of the bed, his legs twitched occasionally and his chest heaved with every breath. Sometimes he paused mid-snore as if he'd run out of air before resuming.

His dog, like his master, had collapsed in a heap on the small bundle of straw near the door. He farted continuously, like the sound of a limp half-full balloon punctured with a needle. The door was locked from the inside with a key that Mr. Jacob had made sure to hide before he lost consciousness. I'd searched every inch of the place in the dark and came up with nothing. My only chance of escape was either in the early morning hours when he was still groggy or once he was sufficiently drunk. I didn't know if I could wait for the latter.

Sometime this morning Lord Henry would be leaving for the hunt and if I wasn't able to get to him in time he would die. Part of me wanted to stay angry at him for allowing this to happen but I couldn't. Even to my own ears, the planted evidence against me was persuasive. Despite what I might or might not be to him I knew what he meant to me. I could not allow him to die. Miss Crabtree's warning to leave things 'as they were' did echo through my mind, but surely I could be afforded this one exception.

So for now, I sat uncomfortably in the wooden rocking chair, mulling over the words in Miss Crabtree's letter and plotting my escape.

At some point I must have fallen asleep because I woke to the sound of meat frying in a pan. Mr. Jacob reluctantly agreed to let me use the outhouse in the backyard but he stayed outside to feed the chickens and unearth another bottle of golden liquid from a hidden stash.

Dense fog had settled in during the night and now visibility was next to nil. The sun had yet to rise, so with any luck he'd drink himself into oblivion before breakfast.

What was in this for him? The countess must have given him a pretty penny to take me off her hands. But how long was he expected to keep up this charade? Maybe until Henry was married. Did she consider me that much of a threat?

During these early morning hours, Mr. Jacob watched my every move. Outside, the fog drifted like smoke over the pasture. The air felt thick with anticipation. As the minutes ticked by and I felt no closer to my departure, panic crept along my conscience.

The thought of attacking Mr. Jacob did cross my mind, but while he was a short man he was incredibly muscular and would bludgeon me before I even threw the first punch. The confines of the small space felt smaller by the second. Having no doubt been raised in a barn himself, by the looks of him, Mr. Jacob was as attuned to my nervous energy as any animal would be and his own instincts were heightened.

"Would ya stop fidgeting, lass?"

"Sorry." I wondered whether I'd even be able to find my way in the thick fog should I get away.

"If you've got energy to burn then I can relieve you of some of it." He jeered at me with rotten teeth and my heart flipped at the violent turn his mood had taken.

Even when my father drank he was never violent, just neglectful. The night usually culminated in me struggling to help him sway to bed.

"No, I'm good."

Once again I wished that an invisibility spell was real and not just in stories. I avoided eye contact like you did with aggressive dogs, hoping that would serve to calm his interest. Other than the dull gray light coming from the window, the only other light in the cabin came from an oil lamp on the bedside table, making the room feel claustrophobic.

"I've no doubt that you're good." He stood and adjusted himself. "I only wonder how you'll look on top of me cock." He laughed, clearly arousing himself with his dirty words.

My heart was beating so fast that I could virtually feel it trying to break out of my chest. "Please don't." But my protest was ignored as he started to sway towards me.

I was armed with nothing but my book. The worst I could do was give him a paper cut. I did a quick scan of the room and I noticed a small cast-iron pan ten paces away. If I dashed…

But the thought must have been written all over my face, because he looked the way my eyes went and blocked my path. There was nowhere to go. I dashed to one side just to avoid having him grab me where I stood and his stubby, dirty hand caught the back of my hair and I crashed to the floor.

"You have no right to touch me," I yelled and tried to get up before the next blow.

"I have every right. I am your husband, remember?" He laughed at this.

"That's a lie." I was on my feet and he was circling me now, trying to figure out the best way to proceed, as I was clearly not going down without a fight.

"I'd have done it for free if I'd known how bonny ya were." He licked his lips as if anticipating a delicious meal and then made a move to catch me.

I dodged him and was now using a chair as a shield.

"Yes, well, I'm sure the countess paid you well, but once Lord Henry finds out you'll be in serious…"

His laughing cut me off.

"Aw, it wasn't the countess who paid me, it was her daughter. A wicked lass, she is," he said with admiration.

"What? Isobel?" My whole body went numb. How could that be?

"Lady Pembrooke, to the likes of you."

With my guard down from the shock, he shot forward and disarmed me of my chair, grabbing me before I could dodge him again. His arm closed tight around my arms and body like a vice. My legs were no longer touching the ground and I kicked violently at anything they could touch. The smell of cheap whiskey and bad hygiene was enough to make me gag. His forehead cracked me hard in the face, most likely breaking my nose and nearly knocking me out completely.

With little effort he flung me down on his bed. The metallic taste of my own blood filled my mouth. Excruciating pain made my eyes sting and face throb. A woozy feeling came over me and threatened to pull me into the dark. His body fell on me hard, pinning me under his weight.

"Well, yer not much to look at now, but no matter." He caught his breath from the exertion of our struggle. At this moment I realized that he would rape me. I had given a good fight but the shock of it and the violence paralyzed me. Never in my life had I imagined that this would happen to me.

Chapter 28

Life or Death

I flashed back to all the times April's father had warned us to be careful when we went into Hollywood together. April and I used to laugh at his protectiveness. Nevertheless, we never walked down dodgy roads at night, always sticking to more populated areas. We even took some self-defense classes, each taking turns to be the assailant. April always liked to play the 'pervert with the puppies,' as she used to joke, and I would pretend to be a Ted Bundy sort of bad guy, the one you didn't see coming.

None of the roleplaying had ever prepared me for this. My heart thumped hard, making it difficult to breathe or even think straight. Adrenaline pumped through my body with such intensity that I could scarcely feel my limbs. Pungent smells of soiled sheets assailed my nostrils and threatened to overwhelm me.

Mr. Jacob's dirty, sausage-like fingers poked between his legs as he tried to release his eager member. I was not ready to accept my fate and give up the fight. My knee rose up hard between his legs and he gasped.

"You bitch!" he spat and his open palm crashed against my face.

My right hand broke free and I grabbed the only thing within reach: an oil lamp on the bedside table. With every bit of strength I could summon I smashed the lamp hard on his head, covering him in oily flames.

His body erupted in fire and went limp. I shoved hard and wiggled out from underneath him. My right sleeve dotted with fire and I dropped to the ground and rolled.

The flames were spreading quickly. I threw a dusty blanket over Mr. Jacob's body but now the whole cabin was a tinderbox ready to go up. Without any water, I couldn't control the fire as it quickly engulfed the furniture.

I dashed for the door, but of course it was locked. The dusty old dog stirred from his straw bed and started to waddle around anxiously.

The key!

Where was it? Had he hidden it somewhere? With the light from the fire I ran around trying to find it but it was useless. The air was already difficult to breathe and soon I would pass out myself from the fumes. With the cast-iron pan I smashed at the wooden shutter until the wood splintered enough to break it open.

Farting from the excitement, the dog circled my feet. Of course I couldn't leave the helpless thing so I scooped him up in my arms. He yelped and tried to nip but I shoved him through the small opening.

The sound of the fire had risen to a roar. What did I do about Mr. Jacob, my jailer and attempted rapist? Part of me was satisfied letting him burn for what he had done, but the other part, the one which nagged continually at my conscience, could not allow a man to die like this, no matter how vile he was. With an eye-rolling sigh, I ran to the bed and tugged as hard as I could, sending him tumbling to the ground with a thump.

The fire had climbed the walls and soon the ceiling would be compromised. With all my strength I dragged his limp body as far as the window, heaving and coughing from the smoke.

Lifting the small dog through the window was one thing but I could never manage a grown man. I slapped him hard to see if I could get him up, but it was useless. He was unconscious. Now the smoke was thick and with each passing second it became more difficult to breathe. I had to leave now. I jumped onto the chair and pulled myself through the small window, landing on soft dirt outside. The old dog had hardly moved from where he'd landed and gave me one single lick of gratitude.

With the dog in hand, I hurried away from the house towards the small farmyard. When I put him down he tried to waddle back towards the house, no doubt in search of his master, but I stopped him and tied him to a fence post with a piece of rope.

At this point I collapsed. Tears and blood flowed from my face, dripping onto my white top like a Jackson Pollock painting. Despite Mr. Jacob's wretched manner, I felt ill leaving a man to his death. I knew these horrific events would take time for me to work through but that would have to wait. I wasn't sure what upset me more: my near rape, near death by fire, the taking of a man's life, Isobel's betrayal and then there was Lord Henry. My anger towards those who had betrayed me now paled in light of the realization that soon Lord Henry would take his last breath. This thought catapulted me into action. I could not allow myself to succumb to shock.

I needed to get away from this place as soon as possible. There was a trough of water for the horses that I used to wash off the damage to my face. Using a rough burlap sack, I gently patted it dry. Its coarse fibers felt like a Brillo pad. My nose had stopped bleeding and I wondered if it had been broken after all.

Within minutes I had tacked up Mr. Jacob's bay gelding and stocked a saddlebag with anything I could find that might be useful. A knife, some rope—my dad always felt that you should have rope in your car so I always got in the habit of it—a half-eaten apple, a dusty blanket and a flask of Mr. Jacob's secret stash, which at this moment sounded better than water.

What to do with the dog? I couldn't just leave him tied to a post, he would likely die of starvation. But he was pretty old anyway. As if on cue he looked up at me with his sad old-dog saggy eyes and all reason was shot to hell. I scooped up the little nippy thing and laid him on the pommel of the saddle in front of me when I mounted.

"Well, I suppose you've never ridden a horse, have you?" I said to him. His ears were pinned back and his body trembled.

I urged the skittish gelding on and he raced forward, eager to put as much distance as possible between himself and the burning house. We were a rather motley-looking crew traveling with little visibility. By now it was no later than eight in the morning but through the veil of fog it was impossible to see anything. While I had paid close attention when we rode in, I struggled with where to go now. Straight down the lane for maybe ten minutes and then we should hit a larger dirt road—that was if we saw it. Sure enough we came to an intersection.

A lightning storm had broken out in the distance to the right. I could feel a familiar humming in my core. It seemed to be pulling me towards those long fingers of electricity. Should I ride towards them and hope that somehow it swallowed me back to my own time? Back to tomorrow? *Hot steaming showers and twenty-first century comforts.* The hum in my body intensified as I considered this. It would be the easy way out. Leaving all this behind was an attractive thought. What kind of danger awaited me if I went back to Lord Henry? Isobel and possibly even her mother had gone to great lengths to make me disappear, what would they do if I returned? Would I be imprisoned or even hanged for the death of Marc Jacob? *Surely not, right?*

Could I go back to the life I'd had before as if none of this had ever happened?

Miss Crabtree's words rang through me. 'Leave things just as you found them, exactly as you found them.' Could I do nothing and just let Henry die?

No. I couldn't do that.

Damn it!

Whatever the ramifications, I was no longer the same girl I'd been even one week ago. Coasting through life was no longer a possibility. I could not allow it. Not this time. Not when I had the power to stop it.

With a tight grip on the little dog, I turned to the left and broke into a canter. The gelding's canter was smooth and steady like a rocking horse. My co-pilot settled in after a minute and stopped panting. When we came alongside the stream we stopped and I allowed the horse to have a quick drink before continuing on.

After what felt like an endless journey, we started to enter countryside that felt familiar. The fog had broken up in parts but continued to float through the forests like smoke on a battlefield. A dusting of drizzle left tiny droplets on my horse's mane that looked like flecks of snow.

What if I was already too late? I couldn't allow myself to think of the what ifs. In this moment, nothing mattered more than getting to Henry.

My arm had grown numb from holding the little dog. The gelding too was starting to tire. With the road to the White Hart in sight, my spirit lifted. I knew I was close.

Just when I finally felt encouraged, the heavens opened and the rain came down in large lazy drops.

Chapter 29

Too Late?

"Really?" I said out loud to myself. As if some unseen force had heard this and decided to up the ante, a clap of thunder roared through the trees, spooking the gelding. Was the storm chasing me? The bay shot forward and I lost hold of my co-pilot, who tumbled to the mud and scurried away from the horse's hooves just in time.

"Whoa, boy, whoa." I tried to soothe him but my own body was humming.

The rain fell harder, making it difficult to navigate the muddy path in front of me. I knew I didn't have time to waste dismounting for the dog. I'd come back for him later. If there was a later. Hopefully, nothing would eat him. I thought of the predators back home in Southern California: the mountain lions, coyotes, bobcats and hawks. Any one of those would find him a tasty treat. But what did they have here? Wolves? Were they extinct yet in England? I couldn't remember but I hoped for both our sakes they were. I pressed on through the dense curtain of rain along the same path I'd walked several days ago with Ben.

And then I saw something.

Up ahead, I could barely make out the blurry figure of a man walking with the hint of a limp. He was tall and lean. All my senses burst with excitement.

"Henry!" I screamed and kicked my horse forward.

The man stopped and spun in my direction.

"Emma?" Lord Henry boomed from fifty yards away. His deep voice was unmistakable. It was like music to my ears.

I jumped from my horse and raced towards him, so relieved to find him intact. He was favoring one leg but otherwise looked unharmed. Thank goodness I'd made it in time. My heart soared when I took in his affectionate expression.

Just when I was steps from him, a movement in the dense bush behind his shoulder caught my eye and I noticed in horror the long barrel of a rifle as it pointed in our direction. The shooter was none other than the mild-mannered boy I'd caught Isobel with, William White. In a split second my own senses went from relief to panic.

"Henry, watch—"

My words were drowned out by an almighty explosion.

I leapt towards Henry to shove him from the path of danger. We hit the ground hard as the sound of gunfire echoed through the woods.

My frayed nerves turned my gut in knots. All I could hear was a ringing in my ears and my own ragged breathing as it caught in my throat. With our limbs intertwined, I struggled out from under Lord Henry's weight.

"Henry! Henry!" The urgency in my voice was impossible to conceal. But he didn't answer.

I scanned the forest for Isobel's lover, bracing for another round, and saw only a cloud of smoke which lingered in his wake. He must have run off.

"Henry." I prodded him more forcefully but there was still no response.

In that moment all the air left my lungs in one big whoosh as I took in the limp body of the man I loved. His jacket was soaked from the rain and red pooled beneath him. He'd been shot. Confusion battled logic. What had happened?

"No!" My anguish flooded out like a moan. I cradled his head to my chest. "You can't die. Not now. I tried to get back to you," I yelled at him as tears streamed down my face. It wasn't supposed to happen this way. My lips grazed his forehead. His body was still warm and I left them there, taking in the last of his heat.

My body lurched forward, threatening to expel the meager contents of my stomach. It felt as if the life was being sucked right out of me. I was hardly able to breathe between sobs. It came out of me in turbulent waves and my whole body shook with shock, exhaustion and utter despair.

All this time I'd thought I needed to get back to save him, but had I instead brought this fate upon him? Had this bullet been meant for me? How could Isabel have known I'd escaped? I knew without a doubt I loved this man more than life itself.

"I love you." The words, like soft music, drifted through the blowing leaves and comforted the depths of my soul. Yes, it was true. I loved this man. I supposed I'd known it from the first moment we'd met, the first touch. There had never been anything I could do to stop it, just as sure as I needed air to breathe.

"I love you." This time I heard it more clearly and I looked around with a jolt, wondering if someone was talking to me. Was I now hearing voices? Was Henry's departing soul reaching out to mine? With my eyes closed, I took in the smell of him, the same hint of soap and lavender as I remembered from before. I knew I would never be able to enjoy the smell of that purple flower again. It would forever be tarnished with the memory of loss.

"Did you hear me?" a raspy voice whispered from somewhere

nearby and my head shot up to see where it had come from. Or had I imagined it?

"Ouch!" Lord Henry's corpse said, his eyes suddenly open.

I let go of his head as if it were possessed and screamed.

"Owww." He groaned. "What's wrong?" he asked, wincing in pain.

"Oh, God. Oh, God. I thought you were dead!" Throwing my arms around him, I helped him to sit up. Relief overwhelmed my senses and I clung to him as if he were about to blow away.

"Well, I may be soon if you continue choking me." He tried to loosen my grip.

"Sorry… I just…" Now I started to cry, from relief or shock or both, and made a motion to cover my face. He caught my hands and squeezed them.

"Were you hit?" he asked, his voice barely above a whisper but full of concern. I shook my head. He scanned the forest for any sign of a threat, his own pistol half pulled out as an afterthought to protect us.

"No, but you have!" It was difficult to mask the panic in my voice. "We have to get you some help." His body was contorting to the right and when I pulled back his jacket I saw that his white linen shirt was soaked with blood.

"Help me bandage the wound to stop the bleeding." The rain had slowed to a drizzle. Thunder could be heard in the distance now and I was relieved that the vibration had slowed. The tug I had felt earlier was no more than a tingle in the tips of my fingers. Miss Crabtree's necklace emitted a subtle heat.

"Okay, I brought a few things with me, hold on." Reluctantly I stood up, not wanting to be even a short distance from him, and raced towards my horse. To my surprise, he hadn't ventured too far. Still exhausted from the ride, he was only twenty feet away near the stream below munching weeds. I grabbed the reins and led the gelding towards Henry.

Once I tied the horse off I brought the few supplies from the saddlebags. First I handed Henry the flask of whiskey. He arched his brow and gave me an inquisitive look, but drank from it anyway. His lips pursed as he forced it down.

"Where on earth did you get this? It's dreadful," he complained.

"Don't ask and don't complain. It's the best I could do in a pinch."

Then I cut the blanket into long bandage-like strips with the knife.

"I'm sorry my hands are so cold," I said as I helped remove Lord Henry's jacket and shirt. There was a lot of blood and he was starting to look drowsy.

Please don't die on me now.

Having seen far too many movies, I took the flask from him and poured some of the whiskey over his wound. He grunted and shot me a stern look.

"To kill the germs," I offered.

"Pardon me?" Confusion was written all over his face.

"I'll explain another time." Obviously germ theory was not yet a thing. "For now just focus on staying alive. I don't think I can handle you dying on me again."

"I'll try to oblige, Miss Emma," he said dryly.

"No need to call me miss, just Emma."

"Very well, just Emma." He said with a deadpan expression.

I shot him a look for trying to be funny. Then I bandaged up his torso and tied it off the best I could. He struggled back into his wet jacket.

"Thank you," he said and paused.

"Don't thank me yet. Who knows if it will hold." I was already throwing everything back in the saddlebag.

"Emma, that's not what I'm talking about." He studied me, suddenly serious. "I'm ashamed that I didn't fight for you. I should have trusted you. And yet here you are saving me."

"Henry, what were you doing walking through the forest in the rain? I thought you were supposed to be on a hunt?" I asked.

"I called it off. I was on my way to find you..."

"To find me? Why? What made you change your mind?"

"I needed to know the truth for myself. Emma, I've been such a cad."

"So you didn't believe it?" I didn't trust my own ears. I had imagined he'd turned his back on me.

I pressed my lips to his and kissed him tenderly. His body responded to me.

"Maybe if I'd not fallen from my horse I would have found you sooner. The billet straps on my saddle must have snapped," he said, looking annoyed that he'd not checked his equipment before setting off.

"Your billet straps?" Memories from two nights ago fluttered through my mind as I recalled a conversation I'd mistakenly overheard between two men in the basement near the servants' quarters. Later that same evening, there had also been the men fiddling with something in the tack room. How could I have failed to put all of this together? The presumed hunting accident had always been foul play. But why, when the hunt had been called off, had his attackers still followed through? If Isobel and William were both behind that plot as well, then Henry finding me put them in grave danger of discovery. Had William followed Lord Henry from the house or me from Mr. Jacobs?

"This is much more serious than broken tack. Someone tried to kill you," I said more to myself.

"It appears that way." He said with a hint of sarcasm. His color was now a sickly gray. "I'm not convinced he won't yet succeed."

"No, I mean there was a plot against you. I just realized. I heard men talking the night of the ball and now it all makes sense." Words were flooding out of me in fragments. "You're in danger. I think you still are."

Henry's energy seemed to be fading. He wasn't worried about anything I was telling him. Instead, he looked at me affectionately, like a man who'd had too many cocktails.

"Miss Crabtree told me that you were special and that one day I would need to place my trust in you rather than those close to me." He smiled weakly. "I thought that those were just the ramblings of a woman who'd lost her senses. I was so blind."

I remembered asking him in the pub what Miss Crabtree had said to him that day as she left the apothecary but he had shrugged the question off. How had she known? Or had she meant it in abstract terms? She'd known my secret the moment she met me.

"And now? Do you trust me?" We needed to get out of there quickly but it felt good to hear him say these things, things I'd secretly hoped I'd hear but never dreamt that I would.

"Now I know I was a fool. I love you, Emma, and never wish to be parted from you. That is if you'd accept me."

Was this a proposal? The idea of it made me feel light-headed and excited.

But what about Jane? And Dormer House? I didn't dare believe this wasn't shock talking. I doubted he'd be released so easily from his engagement.

"The moment you left Dormer House, I realized that without you, life was never going to be worth living. I don't need a title or Dormer House. I need you." His energy was fading fast and I realized that if I didn't get him out of here soon he wouldn't have a life to live.

"First, you'll need to know the truth about me." I noticed that Lord Henry was shaking and I started to worry that he might be going into shock. I pulled the remainder of the blanket over his shoulders. "Let's get you out of here and I'll tell you everything."

He nodded. "The White Hart is close by." He tried to lift his arm to point, but found it too painful.

With great difficulty I helped him to his feet. He staggered around a little, balancing on his good leg. Despite his injuries, he swung a long leg up and vaulted onto the gelding's back. It looked graceful, but once up there he braced himself on the horse's neck against the pain. By the time we reached the pub, Lord Henry was hardly able to hold himself up.

It was well before the lunchtime rush and already a few locals sat with pints of ale at the bar. Lord Henry was leaning heavily on me when we walked through the door. Only the man behind the bar, most likely the owner, took any notice of us.

"Do you have any rooms available?" I asked, not wanting to answer his questioning looks.

"Well, this is not that sort of establishment…" Richard Greasly started to say until he recognized Lord Henry. "Holy Mary, what's happened?"

"An accident," I replied curtly, not wishing to get into the specifics here. "Could we trouble you for a room?"

"Certainly, miss." Richard scurried over to help Henry from his wounded side. The few stragglers at the bar glanced uncomfortably at their future earl. "Are you in need of Dr. Bainbridge?"

"No," Henry mumbled. "No doctors, thank you."

Certainly not that imbecile, I thought to myself.

Chapter 30

The Whole Truth

Mr. Greasly was very helpful at getting us everything we needed. He wanted to send word to his wife, who had gone to the shops, but we both insisted he leave her out of it. The last thing we wanted was for her to start gossiping about what had happened before we'd had time to piece together all the facts.

As far as we knew the people involved most likely believed Lord Henry was dead. As for me, it didn't matter. No one would ever believe my account because I'd already been condemned as a thief, not to mention that I was also a woman.

"Your discretion would be most appreciated, Richard," Henry said to the scared-looking pub owner. Mr. Greasly must have been worried that the future earl could die in his establishment because he continuously asked us if the injuries were serious until we politely asked him to leave. While my presence alone in a room with a man was scandalous, the idea of him dying there was of greater concern.

Now with some light I could see the severity of Henry's wounds. Mr. Greasly had left us a few extra oil lamps so I could properly dress Lord Henry's wounds. His face had lost all its color. Fortunately, the bullet had traveled straight through his right side, so there wasn't anything to be fished out. We had also managed to stop the bleeding and with great difficulty Henry was attempting to sew up his own wound. When I had picked up the needle from the wrong side and couldn't figure out how to thread it he'd quickly lost confidence in my abilities.

I had never been any good in home ec at school. It wasn't fair that the girls were forced to sew aprons or make change purses while the boys got to do woodworking. Who knew I would one day need that skill?

"Do you want another sip?" I held a glass of nice brandy to Henry's lips. Mr. Greasly had been kind enough to leave us a bottle.

He had started breathing through his teeth, which told me it was painful.

"Are you sure you don't want me to give it a go?" I asked.

The skepticism in my own voice was answered with a grunt from Henry, which at the moment was his version of a laugh.

"Almost done here." He accepted a quick sip and continued his work. He was truly gifted at this. The stitching on my own arm was smooth and healing nicely.

With a quick nod he gestured for me to cut the thread. Once the bandages were on, color started to return to his face. He was lying on the small single bed and I sat perched on the side of it. His injured leg was elevated with some pillows after I'd insisted it would help.

He studied my face. We both stared at each other, taking everything in. It was the first time since he'd told me he loved me that we'd had enough light to see one another's expression. His brows furrowed.

"What happened to your nose?" In all the craziness of him being dead and then coming back to life we hadn't talked about how I'd come to him in the first place. "Your left eye looks swollen too."

"Oh, right." As if on cue my nose started to throb and a sick feeling rose in my gut. I wasn't sure how to start.

I felt drained from all the lies I'd had to tell over the past week and couldn't do that anymore. If he was going to love me he needed to love all of me. So I told him what Mr. Jacob had done to me and what he'd said about Isobel being the one to hire him.

Henry listened without interrupting me once. He flinched when I described the struggle and near rape. The whole time I spoke he held my hand, gently stroking me with the pad of his thumb, like he was rubbing a small kitten in the furry bit between its eyes. I cried when I told him about leaving Mr. Jacob in the fire. The loss of human life weighed heavily on my conscience, but he looked at me without judgment.

"Emma, I am appalled that I allowed this to happen to you. You were in my care and I failed you. For that I will never forgive myself. I betrayed your trust and yet here you are tending to my wounds when I should be making amends for yours. As for Isobel, I should have warned you about her the moment she turned up at Dormer House." His expression was somber. "I was consumed with my own problems at the time and failed to."

"You could never have known."

"I have always known her nature and should have taken certain precautions. Even as a young girl she was always so manipulative. I think she does it for sport. She once had a poor stable boy sent away after she pretended he'd tried to force himself on her. Everyone knew she was lying but the boy was sent away anyway and the lad's mother died shortly after for heartbreak. Isobel lied about it because she was feeling bored and wanted some attention." Lord Henry looked disgusted as he remembered the incident.

"Didn't you tell anyone?" I asked.

"Of course. I told my father and he refused to believe it because the countess had assured him it was true. A smart man always sides with his wife, my father told me, and that was the end of it."

It started to make sense. Isobel loved to play the victim so she always bent the facts so that people felt sorry for her. How much energy she must expel keeping track of all the lies or half-truths. She'd thrown me a few bones here and there, making me believe she was so kind and generous, all the while plotting to destroy me. But why? For her own amusement? And what about her brother's attempted murder? Clearly she'd had some hand in that.

Then something struck me. "Henry, if you died, who would inherit the earldom? Would it pass to your brother Edmund?"

"No, he's only my stepbrother. It would go to my sister's husband. God help whoever marries her." He looked mortified at the thought.

"Oh, I didn't realize Edmund wasn't your father's son. Then it makes sense. That could be Isobel's motive."

"I never thought of her as an ambitious woman, but clearly I was mistaken. How easily she was able to deceive us all. She is more clever than I ever imagined."

Her tangled web would be difficult to prove.

"If you tell yourself a lie often enough I suppose eventually you start to believe it." As I said it, it struck a nerve and I realized that I had started to convince myself of the lies I'd been telling since I got here.

"However, it doesn't always work." A look of mock guilt crossed Lord Henry's face. "I tried to tell myself that I wasn't falling in love with you but clearly that failed miserably."

He brought my hand to his lips and kissed it. With a small tug he pulled me down to him and we kissed slowly but passionately. My body tingled under his touch. I could feel that familiar pull he had over me. Soon I would lose myself to him completely, so I pulled away, which took every ounce of willpower I could muster.

Before anything more could be said between us he needed to know the truth about me. I had a new set of butterflies in the pit of my stomach this time, not from need of him but from fear. How was he going to react to what I told him?

"I need to tell you my story."

"You have already, and I'm moved by your courage." He tried to urge me closer.

"No, there's more." I sat up straight and held his hand.

"Oh?" He tried to sit up too but it was too painful so he stayed where he was.

"So you remember the day you found me?"

He nodded. Then I proceeded to tell him everything. When I told him about Ben, I could feel him tense up a little but he listened to my every word. I even told him about my journey into Oxwich alone and about Miss Crabtree.

"Really? Women are allowed to marry each other?" he said with astonishment. After everything I had told him, that was the first thing he picked up on as being a stretch of the imagination.

"You did hear everything I told you, right?" I wasn't sure if he'd actually registered the rest of my story.

"Every word of it." He studied the pattern of the bedding a moment, no doubt trying to figure out what to say. "Well, your story sounds as fantastical as one of those Grimm Brothers' tales. Had you told me this when we'd first met, I'd have known you to be mad. However, knowing you as I've had the pleasure to do so, I can see that you have all your faculties." He laughed a little. "You are nothing like the women I have known in my lifetime, but everything I find myself desiring to be with. I can't fault you for misleading me, as we both know I would never have listened."

"Do you believe me?"

"I do believe that you are telling me the truth as you know it to be. But you'll have to bear with me, Emma, as you've just turned my world upside down in every way." He searched my eyes. "Your story does at least help to explain one small piece of the puzzle."

He dug around in his pocket and pulled out something the size of a business card and handed it to me. I flipped it over in my hand and there was my own face staring back at me. My California driver's license.

"How'd you—?"

"After you'd left, or been taken, I should say"—he looked a little sheepish—"I questioned Harris about your things and after many threats and much persuasion he gave it to me. First he tried to ask for money in exchange but then thought better of it. It turns out he'd been stashing some of our household items in the passageway to the barn in the hopes of fetching a small fortune."

I remembered the candlestick that I'd tripped over in the tunnel.

Henry squeezed my hand. Harris had probably hoped to blackmail me to get it back until he'd realized that I had nothing. I guessed Harris had probably written the note that I'd found under my door.

"He doesn't know how to read"—*or maybe not*—"so I don't think he knew what to make of it. I couldn't make sense of it either at the time, but now, hearing your story..." Henry was still confused but knew that I was telling the truth.

"This is my driver's license." I held it up for him to see. "In my time we don't get around on horseback or carriages, we have cars. It's like a carriage but with a motor instead of horses. It propels itself forward and it goes very fast."

"Incredible," he said with the fascination of a little boy. "What about those germs you spoke of? Is that something from your time?"

I wasn't sure how much I should say. Was this going to disrupt something in the space-time continuum? Was that even a thing?

"Germs are like tiny little bugs that we can't see with our eyes but that transmit disease. In the near future one of your physicians will discover the germ theory and then it will become widely known. Just like cholera. A physician named John Snow is right now investigating the cholera outbreak in London and will soon discover that contaminated water is the source."

"If what you say is correct, we've had it all wrong." He smoothed his left hand through his hair as he contemplated what I'd just told him, his interest in medicine taking hold.

"Obviously I'd keep this to yourself. I don't know how this knowledge could affect anything in the future."

"If you are truly what you say you are"—he hesitated—"from the future, do you want to go back?"

Ah, the question I'd been asking myself. His eyes were searching mine. It felt like they were pleading with me to say no.

"Well, I did at first, but I didn't know how. I'm still not clear on how I got here. But now…" We looked at each other and I realized this was where I belonged. With him.

A loud knock at the door startled both of us. I could hear voices on the other side. Mrs. Greasly was fussing over someone.

"Out of my way, woman!" It was the muffled sound of the earl's voice.

The door swung open. In poured the earl, flanked by two men in blue uniform, both looking like they'd been dragged out of bed or come straight from a long night of drinking. Mrs. Greasly flitted about trying to reassure everyone that they were operating a decent establishment and not a brothel. Her eyes fell on me with accusation.

"Constable, arrest this woman for attempting to harm my son. And for the murder of Mr. Marc Jacob." The earl practically spat the words. I stood up immediately in all the panic.

"Father, this is ridiculous!" Lord Henry shouted, trying to get out of bed, but found that his body was far less mobile than he thought. "You're gravely mistaken."

"This woman is a thief and a charlatan," the earl continued.

"You're wrong!" I shouted back. "Someone tried to kill your son and if I'd not come along they'd have succeeded."

"How dare you talk to me with such incivility. You may have corrupted my son's better judgment but not mine. Remove this woman from my sight immediately."

"You have no right." Lord Henry was furious. "Miss Emma is not the villain here, it is Isobel and your wretched wife! If you so much as displace one hair on her body, so help me, I will strike you down." His eyes were bloodshot, making him look more fierce, and everyone in the room held their breath to see what the earl would do next.

The storm outside had come back with a vengeance and a clap of thunder had everyone a little more tense. All eyes were on me, as if I'd used special powers to summon the storm. Everyone seemed on edge. Mrs. Greasly made some little hand gesture against the devil. Part of me wanted to laugh at the absurdity, but when men had their dander up who knew what could happen with the least bit of provocation. Like fighting dogs, a change in the breeze could be enough to turn the tide.

"Take her." The earl would not look weak in front of an audience. Whatever storm might come from it, he didn't care as long as he didn't lose face right now.

One short burly constable grabbed hold of me from behind and dragged me out of the room. I would not be falsely imprisoned. Not again. Not this time.

"No!" Lord Henry shouted from the room. "Release her!"

"Constable, I need to teach my son a lesson, if you'll excuse us."

My legs thumped down the stairs as my captor tried to drag a woman taller than himself. I only pretended to struggle weakly until we were down the stairs and away from the watchful eyes of the other constable. The bear hug was the easiest grab for a woman to escape from if she knew what to do and it just so happened I did. April and I had loved our kickboxing and street-fighting classes. We'd done them during college more as exercise, never imagining that we would ever use it for real.

As soon as I was alone with my assailant I dropped my weight down into a squat and raised my arms at the biceps. When his grip loosened I swung my right leg and hip back and with my left arm shoved his torso backwards so that we both collapsed to the ground. He hit his head hard when we came down and I jumped up and ran out the door before he realized what had happened.

The rain was bucketing down once again and I ran towards the stable where the gelding was sheltered under the eaves. My heart was racing, thumping hard in my throat. With a flying leap I attempted to vault onto his back. A sharp pain shot up my pubic bone as I missed my mark, but I kicked him forward anyway. He lunged into a fast trot and then a long smooth canter. My only thought was to get away, but as soon as we were a fair distance away I had to figure out where to go.

Miss Crabtree.

She seemed to be the only safe place for me. It was incredibly gloomy, but when I came out of the forest on the top of a rolling hill overlooking a quarry, I could make out lights in the distance. It had to be Oxwich. They stretched out for a long way. A part of me felt reluctant to keep going. I hated putting so much distance between myself and Henry. At least for the moment he was safe.

I dug my heels in and rode towards the lights. Another deafening thunderclap came right on top of us this time and the whole sky lit up like the Fourth of July. The smell of sulfur stung my nose and a sickening vibration coursed through my body. My horse stumbled and I slid off his back, crashing to the ground in a somersault.

Everything went black.

Chapter 31

Despair

Beep, beep, beep came the annoying sound. It was low but grated on my every nerve. Like the bleep of an alarm clock. My head throbbed. The bile rose up in my throat and I turned my head just in time to retch. My body heaved and I threw up again. Someone shuffled around my room and when I opened my eyes Ben looked down at me with a look of concern.

"What the…?" were the first words that came to me. I wasn't sure if I said them out loud or if I just thought them.

"Nurse!" Ben called out and looked towards the door. I was in a hospital room.

I was stunned, unable to even utter a word. A surly nurse with red wispy hair came waddling in. For a moment my heart leapt when I thought it was Miss Barnsby but it was just a partial doppelganger.

"Yes, son? Oh, has she been sick again?" She clucked with sympathy.

She cleaned everything up.

"The doctor'll be in in a bit, dear." She said this like I was hard of hearing, then looked to Ben. "It'll be all right, you'll see."

No, nothing is all right.

"Emma, can you hear me?" Ben was trying hard to be brave.

All I could do was blink my eyes in confirmation. My lips had lost the will to even open. What had happened to me? Where was Henry?

Chapter 32

Déjà Vu

While the doctor spoke I caught only every fifth word. It was like Charlie Brown listening to grown ups. Wah, wah, wah… temporal lobe seizure… wah, wah.

I knew I should be listening. Ben was doing that for the both of us. Right now I was processing. Once again my whole world had been turned upside down just when I was starting to feel like I had my feet under me. My lips still buzzed from my last kiss with Henry like it was only moments ago.

Ben looked at me just then and I wondered if he knew what I was thinking. I couldn't even muster up enough emotion to feel ashamed. The last thing I remembered was sliding off the gelding's back when the lightning struck and then everything went black.

"It's very common for someone suffering these types of seizures to feel confused and possibly even angry when they come out of it." The doctor's white coat glowed from the sunlight, making him look like an apparition. Perhaps he was just that. "The MRI we did early is consistent with TLE." He clicked a wireless mouse and a picture of my brain filled the screen on the wall.

"You see here?" He pointed to a spot on my brain. Like a bored teen, I only half cocked my head to follow what he was doing. "This section looks smaller and brighter."

Ben asked a question, good student that he was, but I stopped listening. I didn't want the doctor's medical explanations. How could he tell me everything I'd been through was only a symptom of epilepsy? I didn't have epilepsy, not that I knew of.

When I'd tried to explain how real and vivid everything was to me both he and Ben simply looked at each other with a silent nod, like they were in on a secret. It infuriated me. That was when I stopped listening. I'd gone through something. I was a Wayfarer! It was a thing!

"It could be from head trauma she may have suffered in an incident long ago that no one noticed at the time. We can't be sure," the doctor was explaining to Ben as if I wasn't even in the room.

"What about the car that hit me on my bike?" I suddenly felt like I needed to pay attention. Both men looked my way like they'd only just noticed me there.

"What do you mean? When were you hit by a car?" Ben looked confused.

"Well, that's how all this started, isn't it? I went to get groceries on Mrs. Grimshaw's bike and when I left the store it was raining hard and some car plowed into me."

Both the doctor and Ben looked to each other as if they were now dealing with a crazy person. My blood started to boil.

"When did this happen?" Ben asked skeptically.

"I don't know, a week ago. I don't even know what day it is, but that's when I hit my head."

"Darling"—Ben was trying to be soothing now—"you haven't been gone for a week. We found your bike yesterday. It was by the side of the road but you were nowhere in sight. If you'd been hit, you would have been badly injured and not able to walk away as you did.

Your groceries were left scattered across the street. A man driving by found your phone under one of the plastic bags and called my number because you'd listed it in your emergency contacts. That's how we knew you were in trouble."

"I was zapped into another time. I wasn't just in trouble, I vanished. It was 1854 and I stayed in Dormer House. I could even tell you the name of their butler."

Ben shifted uncomfortably.

"Maybe time works differently there." Even to my own ears the possibility sounded far-fetched. Still, I wasn't ready to give in and it was exhausting trying to convince them.

"Temporal lobe seizures affect your memories and you can often have vivid dream-like sequences that feel very real. You may also experience many déjà vu moments." The doctor was trying to help me understand. "But it doesn't mean these things actually happened."

"But I know they did." Tears of frustration stung my eyes but I blinked them back. No one here believed me.

"It can certainly feel that way," the doctor said. "The drugs we have you on will help with these symptoms and we're hopeful that if you respond to them you won't need surgery."

Nothing made sense anymore. How had an entire week just not happened? Henry. My gut twisted at the loss of him. He had touched my soul more deeply than I had ever experienced and now I was to believe that that had not happened? That the whole experience was just a symptom of some condition?

The sobs started without warning. My body convulsed with anguish for the loss I felt. Ben tried to put a hand on my shoulders to console me, but I barely noticed it. My skin felt numb with despair. My crying was a slobbery mess, with sharp racking breaths followed by embarrassing moans, the kind where dribble fell from my mouth. I didn't care that the two men stood staring at me and that more than one nurse came in to ogle. I just didn't care. My world had fallen apart and I didn't even have the energy to worry who watched on the sidelines. How could they possibly understand?

"Most people have completely normal lives, Emma. Like I said, you could respond very well with the drugs." The doctor looked to Ben, who was a bit shell-shocked himself. Ben had seen me cry many times but never completely break down as I was doing.

"I think Em just needs a moment to process all of this," Ben told the doctor, who nodded in agreement and made a motion to leave before turning back to Ben.

"I'll let you know when we have all the results from the blood tests," the doctor said just before closing the door.

Ben looked like he was afraid of me. This was not what he had signed on for.

Eventually, exhaustion took over and I passed out.

Chapter 33

Belong

I woke up to the sound of whispering. When my eyes finally opened, I saw the doctor talking to Ben quietly in the corner.

"What I don't understand is how she managed to make it all those miles in her condition," Ben said. "Police had already searched that whole area. It was as if she just appeared out of thin air."

"Judging by her broken nose, she may have fallen quite hard. Could have been enough to knock her out. I suspect that she felt disorientated, wandered off and then simply collapsed in the field. She may not have been visible from the road. We know how thorough our country coppers can be," the doctor said with no small amount of English sarcasm. "That would certainly explain why she wasn't found sooner."

Ben caught my eye and coughed to alert the doctor that I was listening.

"Oh, you're awake." The doctor turned his attention to me.

"What were you guys talking about?"

"I was just mentioning to the doctor how, after you'd fallen, you'd wandered off quite a distance." Ben looked anxiously to the doctor. "I wasn't sure how you'd managed that, given your broken nose and apparent disorientation."

"How far was it?" I asked out of curiosity.

"Nearly ten miles. You were all the way up that ridge by the limestone quarry overlooking Oxwich. Do you know why you were heading that way instead of towards our cottage, which was only a few miles away?"

The only explanation I could come up with I knew they would never accept. Why was I on that ridge? Because I had been running for my life when the world had swallowed me up and spat me back into my own time.

"Ben, I heard you say that the police were looking for me."

"We were all looking for you," he cut in.

"How long exactly was I missing?"

"Six hours," he replied sheepishly. "With the rain and all, we didn't know which way you'd gone."

It was as if a small flame had suddenly ignited within me, giving me a sliver of hope where there had been none. That had to be something, right? Ben had said it was as if I had appeared out of thin air. That was how Lord Henry had described it too. I could picture the exact spot on the ridge he was talking about. At the time, the lights of Oxwich had been a welcome sight. How else could you explain why I was found there? I had been there when I crossed back into the future. Maybe I wasn't crazy.

"The good news is you were found and now you're free to go." The doctor was checking his watch as if eager to make his last rounds before he slipped away for the evening. "We have a few test results we're still waiting on, but you can make an appointment to come in tomorrow and we can go over them in my office. I'll give you a prescription for some painkillers in addition to your medication. It should ease any discomfort you might be feeling."

I highly doubt that.

"Okay, you're sure she can leave?" Ben looked nervous at the prospect of being in charge of me. "You don't need to keep her for observation?"

I no longer wanted to waste any more time. Where had I really been for those six hours? Did one hour here equal one day there? Did time move at different speeds? All I knew was that there was still a possibility, however slim, that I hadn't imagined the whole thing. First, I would need some proof. Anything to corroborate my recollections.

Ben was eyeing me as if waiting for me to erupt. I could tell he was worried about bringing me home. Conversations needed to be had, but not here. It would not be easy to break off the engagement. Of course it was the right thing to do, but I hated the idea of hurting him. In the long run I knew it would be for the best. Everyone deserved to be loved. I understood that now.

"No, that won't be necessary..."

A stout little nurse knocked at the door and popped her head in.

"Ruth!" The doctor waved her in and then turned his attention back to us. "The nurse will go over your medication. I'll see you tomorrow for your follow up." Adjusting his files in one hand, the doctor left my room briskly.

"Hello, luv." Ruth handed me a plastic bag. "Here are your things. Your clothes are a bit torn but I've had them cleaned."

I pulled my white top from the bag and something dropped to the floor with a thud. Ben bent down to pick the object off the floor.

"When did you get this, Em?" He handed it over to me.

It was the black stone necklace that Miss Crabtree had given me. I traced its familiar sharp edges. Now I had my proof. I had traveled to another time. Despite all the evidence against it, it was possible and I was living proof.

"Is it yours?" Ben looked confused.

"No, I borrowed it from a friend," I said, feeling a smile tug at the corners of my mouth. "I'll need to return it." The meaning of my words was lost on Ben but in my own head the cogs were cracking into gear. "Do you think we could stop in and see Dormer House before going home?"

He gave me a funny look. Maybe walking through, I would find some other bit of proof that I'd been there.

"Why would you want to go there? It's just ruins. There's not much to see." He was in the middle of packing up his bag with his computer and work stuff.

"Dormer House? In ruins?"

"Yes, it burnt down over a century and a half ago. You knew that, Em."

"Right, of course." The shock was almost palpable but I didn't let it show. Something I had done had changed more than just one man's fate.

What had happened after I'd left?

What had become of Lord Henry?

But the real question which tugged at me with every fiber of my being was…

What was I going to do about it?

Thank you for reading

The Wayfarer!

I hope you enjoyed it. I'm always grateful for reviews. If you'd like to share your thoughts, comments or feedback, you can always reach me by email: jlhayesauthor@gmail.com

Find me on Twitter (jenl_hayes) or
Facebook (jenniferlhayes)
where you can join my mailing list.

20930901R00137

Printed in Great Britain
by Amazon